THE LAST GO-DOWN

Joe Pilgrim was back at the home ranch — but not for long! A friend of his had been savagely murdered and a handsome killer and his gang were on the run. And so the troubleshooting gunfighter was forced to hit the retribution trail once more. An old love waited in sorrow for Pilgrim and a new one wondered whether this could be the last go-down. Soon men would die in a brutal double-cross, and in the borderlands an ancient reprobate sought stolen gold and a new chance.

JAY HILL POTTER

THE LAST GO-DOWN

Complete and Unabridged

LINFORD
Leicester

First published in Great Britain in 1998 by
Robert Hale Limited
London

First Linford Edition
published 2001
by arrangement with
Robert Hale Limited
London

British Library CIP Data

Potter, Jay Hill
  The last go-down.—Large print ed.—
Linford western library
  1. Western stories
  2. Large type books
  I. Title
  823.9'14 [F]

ISBN 0–7089–4582–1

ULV 31.7.01

Published by
F. A. Thorpe (Publishing)
Anstey, Leicestershire

Set by Words & Graphics Ltd.
Anstey, Leicestershire
Printed and bound in Great Britain by
T. J. International Ltd., Padstow, Cornwall

EH0901

Part One

Grim Return

1

The young man on the smart pinto had planned to go straight to the ranch which was his destination. He could see the roofs of the town in the near distance to the right of him and then he realized he was climbing. On the rise near to the Boot Hill, he saw the people and said, 'Hold it, pard,' and the horse stopped.

The morning sun was coming up and the folks on the hill were black etchings, a lot of them for such an early time.

The young man saw the hearse and the horses and said, 'Let's take a look, pard.' He signalled with a jerk of the reins and the horse slanted off, climbing again but at a different angle.

They were almost atop the rise when the old man saw them.

He had always had hawk-eyes in his hawk-like face.

The younger man had known that the old man's trouble was plaguing him again. But not this bad. On two sticks, but managing to smile in surprise.

'Hallo, Dad,' he said not letting his own surprise and concern show on his poker face.

'Hallo, Joe. Didn't expect you so soon.'

'Didn't expect to see you in this place, old-timer. What's going on?'

The old man didn't answer the question. He had leonine grey hair curling thickly from beneath a black slouch hat. He was all in black.

He said, 'I was told you might be coming, but I didn't really expect you yet. I also heard that you had a woman. I figured that when you came maybe you'd have her with you, be married even, ready to settle down.'

'She's back in the borderlands where I met her, Dad. She was fine. A good girl. But she wasn't the one for me.'

The old man said, 'Dan Profett is dead. Murdered. This is his buryin'. I'm glad you got here on time.'

'I didn't know, of course. I'm mighty sorry.'

The two were joined by a young couple, the girl younger than Joe, the man of about the same age. Joe was down from his horse. The girl kissed him and he called her 'Sis'. He shook hands with the tall quiet man who was his brother-in-law.

The empty hearse, the erect, black-hatted driver up front behind the four black horses, was going down the hill back to town. Folks on foot trailed behind. There were a few scampering kids.

Nobody else joined the two young men, the old man and the girl, though a few covert glances were thrown in their direction. A couple of men saluted from a distance and the greeting was returned by young Joe.

The old man and his daughter and son-in-law had been with friends who were now moving off, not wanting to intrude on a family reunion. They would later pay their respects to the new arrival, the old man's son.

And now the Pilgrim clan were together again. Ex-marshal now rancher Joe Pilgrim Senior, still known by many as 'Marshal Joe', his daughter Rebbie and her husband Cal who was also ranch foreman.

And last, but very far from least, was young Joe, notorious gunfighter, bounty-man and sometime lawman as his father had been. Young Joe came and went: 'twas said that this was the second visit he'd made since Marshal Joe had been involved in the incident about which folks still talked and which had caused the old ex-lawman to walk on sticks from time to time.

'I'll go get the buggy,' Cal said. 'Then I'll ride your horse, Joe. You get up with your dad and Rebbie and they can tell you what's been going-down round here lately. All right?'

'All right.'

⋆　⋆　⋆

Dan Profett had been long-time head teller at the local bank which was owned by his old friend Silas Tagwell, though their relationship had been somewhat strained in recent times due to the machinations of Silas's only offspring, his no-good son, Michael.

Silas could see no wrong in Michael, or pretended he couldn't. Money had gone missing from the bank and Michael had pointed the finger at old Dan, was supposed to have found proof. Michael's two pards, called Ripper and Dack, had backed him up: they knew the truth of it they said. They followed Michael in everything like twin tails of a wild kite. They were as bad as he was. But could anybody be as bad as young Michael was, some folk asked? Maybe he'd somehow been spawned by a rattlesnake than by his sainted mother who had died giving him birth.

Silas Tagwell had worshipped that woman, hadn't been the same man after losing her, doted on Michael in her stead, though maybe some men would have done just the opposite and sort of blamed the lad. He was so much like his mother — in looks that was. But that was all. He was a real bad one.

Marshal Joe said, 'Dan and Silas had a showdown and Dan walked out of the bank, didn't go back. And Silas didn't ask him to, backed his damn' son all the way. Certainly no missing money was found and no proof against Dan, far as I know. Things came to a head in a sudden and terrible way, Joe . . . '

The old man's voice tailed off. His son, known mainly the length and breadth of the wide Southwest merely as 'Pilgrim', asked, 'Did Silas call the law in?'

'No, he didn't go that far. But his son went much further.'

Rebbie, who hadn't spoken since the three of them had got in the buggy and Marshal Joe had taken the reins, now said in a soft, sad voice, 'It was a terrible thing.' And then her father told the rest of the story.

He began by saying that Michael

Tagwell seemed to have gone loco. The old lawman's son said he had always figured that Michael wasn't quite right in the head, that there were too many of his kind in the territories nowadays, many of them younkers and from all walks of life, human scum who thought they could get away with anything.

2

By the time Marshal Joe and his son-in-law heard about Dan Profett's murder the sheriff and posse had gone out. Old Joe told his son that his pard Tim Molan had gone with the posse.

Young Joe said, 'I ain't seen Tim for years. How is he? I hope he doesn't stick his fool neck out too far.'

'He'll be all right. He doesn't change. He's sittin' pretty in the stores his folk left him.'

'I didn't know he'd lost his folks.'

'There's a lot you don't know, bucko. Tim married your old sweetheart, Ruthie. Did you know that?'

'No.'

'Yeh. You three were always together when you were tads, weren't you? But you went fiddlefootin' and Tim stayed put.'

'I guess I'll go see Tim; Ruthie

anyway, if Tim ain't back.'

'He'll be back. I reckon them killers have got a mighty start on the posse. And they can't chase 'em forever, can they?'

Dan Profett had been left in an alley, done to death by Michael Tagwell and his partners-in-crime.

It looked like Dan had caught them rifling the bank. It appeared that Michael, after doing it before in smaller ways, was throwing discretion to the four winds and going for the big boodle at last, didn't aim to wait for an inheritance, was aiming to do a long pasear.

Old Dan, however, hadn't been the only one who'd spotted the four. A drunk called Hicks had been half-asleep in a nearby alley, had crouched, half out of his wits, seen the action, hadn't been spotted himself.

Seemed like Dan Profett had been keeping tabs on Michael, but he'd gotten too close and had paid for that with his life.

On hearing the news, Michael's father, Banker Silas Tagwell, had suffered a heart attack, was still struggling for his life. The local doc, an old friend, was mightily worried about him.

Silas wasn't a bad man. Misguided maybe. But no shark.

Dan Profett and Silas Tagwell had been friends for years before the accusations had been levelled at the former. Silas had not only lost an old friend, but virtually his own son also, couldn't cover for the boy any more, not even in his now-sick mind.

Young Joe Pilgrim said, 'I remember well Dan Profett's missus. After Mom died, Miz Profett was like an aunt to me an' Rebbie.'

'She was,' agreed Joe's sister.

'They had a son, too, didn't they?' said Joe. 'Called Luke. A quiet boy. Me an' him were never actually pardners.'

Old Marshal Joe said, 'He went East. Got rich I guess. Dan didn't say.'

'He wouldn't. As I remember, him

an' his missus loved that boy mightily. The only one. Like the banker's Michael. Luke might have run off, but he was no Michael. Maybe after they lost his ma he missed her too much.'

'Maybe,' said Marshal Joe, giving his son a shrewd sidelong glance. There was still understanding and compassion in the innards of this outwardly hardbitten young man. There was hope for him yet. Maybe he'd settle down.

The ranch was in sight. 'By cracky, I'm hungry,' Joe said.

'I'll fix you something special, Brother mine,' said Rebbie.

★ ★ ★

Everybody called him Michael. His dad had always called him Michael. He didn't mind being called Michael.

There were enough damn' Mikes about, he thought. Being Michael made him sort of special, a man who could do anything, just anything.

To begin with there'd been three of

them. The usual trio: Michael and his two sidekicks, Ripper and Dack. But that night Ripper and Dack had been drinking with another acquaintance, a hardhat called Benjy and he'd been tagging along. He was good with his fingers, with windows, safes, locked drawers. When they worked on old Dan, Benjy had used the barrel of his gun like a whip, wasn't going to harm those dexterous hands of his.

Well, if he got troublesome they could get rid of him later — one less share of the rich boodle. But right now a posse had to be on their heels and they could use an extra gun.

They were in the foothills when they actually spotted the posse. They counted. Seven. That wasn't a hell of a lot. The sheriff, two deputies, four volunteer townies.

'Let's take 'em,' said Michael.

The posse was in the open, coming fast, but not spread out too much. The sun was hot and there was no breeze.

But now, seeing ambush cover ahead,

the sheriff gave a waving signal with one hand and the riders began to spread the horses out, lessen targets.

The bunch in the hills were already hunkered down with rifles. 'God, he's reading my mind,' Michael said. 'Pick your man. No cross-firing. Take 'em.'

He fired first. A horse screamed, a shrill, agonizing sound on the still air. The beast went down, throwing his rider clear. The other men were lower in their saddles now, harder to hit, coming on fast. They had their handguns ready and were close enough for snapshooting pretty quickly. But the men in the rocks were well covered.

The horseless man was down on his belly in cover of the stout body of his dead mount. He had his rifle from the saddle scabbard and was aiming at the puffs of smoke up there in the rocks. A shooting fool! Covering for his pards anyway.

Bullets thudded into the carcass of the horse. The man had his hat tilted to the back of his head, had as much cover as anybody, certainly more than his friends, though they were getting nearer to the rocks and cover. But then one of them gave a high, keening cry and went backwards out of the saddle as if hit by an invisible fist. His arms waved, and then he hit the ground with a hard impact and didn't roll, lay still, his blood soaking the sparse grass before the rocks began.

His friends were flinging themselves from their horses, seeking cover. But one of them, crouching, ran back to the wounded man who, though badly hurt, a wound in his chest, was moving slightly, trying to drag himself along. The second man, his would-be rescuer, was not even halfway as lucky. He caught a bullet in the back of the head which tore through to his face and pitched him down within a few inches of his wounded friend, both of them with one hand outstretched as if for a last desperate shake. And the wounded man then crawled past the body of his dead friend, was finally helped into cover, shaking his head dolefully from side to side till he passed out and the gunfire no longer rang in his ears.

Up in the rocks Michael was shouting, 'Shoot the goddamn horses.' But the beasts were scattering, hard to hit, and the posse was in cover, except one dead man and one dead horse. The hot sun beat down on the suddenly still and silent scene: a lull in the shooting. Michael was saying, 'All right, let's get outa here then. They ain't in much shape to follow us now, are they?' Nobody argued with him. 'But keep your heads down.' Their horses were nearby. Unharmed, the four men mounted up.

They didn't look back towards the posse, couldn't see them anymore anyway. The big man with the star on his breast said, 'We can't go any further. And the other side of the hills is outa my jurisdiction anyway.' There was fury in his voice, and sadness. They looked at him but nobody else said anything. They knew he was talking tragic sense.

One man dead and another badly wounded, still unconscious, needing toting and then medical attention as soon as possible. A horse dead and the other mounts to be gathered. The men rose wearily and got to it.

3

She had never been what you could call a beauty. Not Ruthie. But she'd been a sweet kid. And she hadn't changed.

She still had a cheerful, chubby face, big brown eyes and a mass of black hair. She'd had the loveliest body Pilgrim had ever seen on female kind, still had that he thought.

She had been the first girl that he'd had a sexual experience with. He wondered if his then best friend Tim had known that.

Ruthie and Tim were married now and, when Pilgrim called, Tim was still off with the posse.

Ruthie was delighted to see her old friend young Joe Pilgrim, but her demeanour was constrained by her sadness about the terrible death that had come to Dan Profett who she said had been like an uncle to her, being her dad's friend and all. Ruthie also, of course, was anxious about her husband, Tim, who'd never been out with a law posse before.

No, Tim's never been a gunfighter, Pilgrim thought, not like me. But wisely he kept those thoughts to himself.

He took coffee with Ruthie. They were both a little pensive. He didn't stay long.

When he got back to the ranch it was to be greeted by more tragic news. Banker Silas Tagwell had died, a hand had just brought in the news.

⋆ ⋆ ⋆

From the front window, Ruthie could see across the town. The light was failing. The sun was like a ball of blood sinking below the rooftops.

She moved to the main bedroom of the sprawling one-storey place. The other odd room was little more than a cubbyhole with just a narrow window, but the main bedroom was spacious and looked out at one of the trails into town — the trail from the hills — with only small shacks and outhouses to spoil the view.

There was nobody approaching along the part of the trail she could see. She was anxious, nervous. She was almost afraid to stand where she was, with one hand on the arm of the chair beneath the window.

She couldn't sit. She peered out, not seeing the sun as she had done over the town. Now there was only a vestige of its red glow.

She forced herself to stand there, erect, staring out as the light failed, knowing that now the sun would be almost hidden, the light becoming less, the shadows lengthening.

She was shakingly afraid when she saw the bunch of horses and men coming along the trail, dim figures bobbing up and down like puppets, becoming slowly clearer to her view. Bigger anyway, but still somewhat hazy. As if her eyes were playing her tricks.

She said, 'Oh!' Half-cry — a thin one. But she forced herself to turn away from the window and move from the bedroom into the sitting-room and across the kitchen and out through the main door. Then she could see part of the main street, and part of the trail, too. People were moving out of the street in the direction of her and the trail.

And then she was ahead of them, running, her hands held out in front of her as if in some kind of supplication.

* * *

After the blazing hot sun there was a danger of rain. The heat was suffocating, but during the night there were only a few storm-spots. The following morning was cloudy and even before the sun came up the humidity was bad.

By the time there was a clearer light the people were gathered on Boot Hill.

Of a sudden, though, the morning clouds began to darken the sky, blanketing the sun. As if there was a pall of death over the town. As if there'd been some kind of massacre and this was the aftermath.

On the hill, people moved like so many ghosts and the hearse and its four black horses were like a mirage.

Two funerals: the burying of Banker Silas Tagwell, and that of the young storeman Tim Molan, whose widow, Ruthie, stood weeping over the open grave till she was led away as the clods began to fall.

News had spread quickly, terribly, and most everybody was here at last.

But there was no sign then of the young manhunter known as Joe Pilgrim.

4

He was on the edge of the Pecos territory, the town, the ranch far behind him. It was still raining, had started not long after he'd left Boot Hill and had continued steadily.

He wore his slicker and had his hat pulled well down over his eyes, though it didn't completely spoil his vision. Anyway, there was nothing to see. The rain formed a grey veil, not a heavy downpour now, a monotonous steadiness.

He had seen a few cows, a few riders moving slowly in the distance. Now there was only the grey veil. He hardly heard the rain, which seemed as if it would go on forever.

A half-drowned rider seated on plodding horse-flesh, he came suddenly upon sight of buildings appearing like a mirage through the rain.

Man and horse, bent, plodding, they saw a small settlement and, as they got nearer to it — and it was real! — they saw the gleam of the river just beyond the buildings.

Maybe the Pecos was shallower at this point. There might even be a bridge.

Pilgrim didn't know whether he'd been on this trail before. He didn't think he recognized the settlement, a conglomeration of shacks with gaps between them that couldn't be called streets.

If there was some kind of river crossing maybe other riders, intent on fording the river, had come here ahead of him. Maybe horses and men had swum as Pilgrim and his mount might have to do. They couldn't get much wetter than they already were.

At first they couldn't see anything moving. This could be a ghost town. But then a door slammed, like a pistol shot. Pilgrim reached downwards to the proximity of his holstered handgun, thus getting his paws tangled in the wet clinging folds of his slicker. A man, head down, running along a sagging board, disappeared through another door. Another slam. And Pilgrim, disgruntled, said, 'C'mon boy.'

Then they heard the noise from behind the door through which the fellow had disappeared. A tinkling piano.

An overhang would partly shelter the horse. Pilgrim left him there and trod on boards and then opening the door, passed through it. He didn't slam it. He moved catlike.

The piano was louder now and there were quite a lot of people. A cantina, a rathskellar: Pilgrim had seen dozens like it. Outside, the rain had killed the heat of the sun, but in here the heat was palpable, and welcoming, and there were a lot of shadows.

Shadows could be comforting, but in places like this Pilgrim was wary of shadows. He paused to get his eyes accustomed to this new half-light and to probe the deeper darknesses. He knew that eyes were on him too. But then he sensed — and saw them — that those eyes had turned away from him after measuring him quickly. Another saddletramp. No doubt many of them passed this way on their trail to the river.

He could see the bar, a shine of glass behind it. He moved forward and folks eased aside to let him through and he murmured thanks.

A big, half-breed barman served him with rye and a cold beer chaser. 'Anyplace I can put my horse, feed him?' Pilgrim asked.

The big man, who looked half Siwash, jerked a big brown thumb. 'Livery stable. Just a short piece.'

He watched admiringly as the young stranger downed his drinks, took a breath, asked, 'Can I get some grub when I come back?'

'Surely, suh. I'll get you a menu.'

A menu no less, thought Pilgrim, as he went through the door and back out into the rain. This place was looking up. And even the skies seemed to be lightening a mite.

'Come on, pizen.'

The pinto gave him a disgruntled look and let himself be led. The small livery table was no great shakes but would surely do, and the wizened oldster in charge was affability itself.

The young stranger broached a few friendly questions after explaining his reason for them. He was looking for some pards of his, four of 'em most likely, who'd be coming this way. He'd hoped to catch up with them by now. He hadn't spotted them in the little saloon down the street, wondered if the livery man had seen them.

The oldster had a shrewd light in his rheumy eyes. 'You a lawman, mister?'

'Hell, no, what makes you think that?'

Right now, truth! And the livery man commented, 'Figured you could handle yourself anyway. Saw those four earlier maybe. Left. Guess they went over the river. About your age. The one who seemed to be the boss-man was kinda fancy. I heard one o' the others call 'im Michael.' The old man gave a little cackle. 'A han'some duck an' all.'

Lady Luck was at last smiling on Pilgrim. Even the rain was abating, though there was no sun; time was getting on, probably there'd be no more sun today anyway.

Pilgrim's early fury had abated. He was looking upon this trail now as many he had taken of a similar nature. A manhunter's trail. He was cool, figuring. He was also very hungry, and kind of tired. His horse needed sustenance and rest also.

The man went back to the rathskellar. The menu was a short list scribbled on a piece of well-fingered cardboard. The Siwash behind the bar recommended the spiced chicken an' extras, so Pilgrim tried it and it wasn't half bad. He'd already washed up at a pump out back. The rain had stopped. The river gleamed in a dying light.

Pilgrim dozed in a chair, ignoring the growing babble around him, the piano starting up again. He had already ascertained from the big, friendly barman that the Pecos River was shallow just ahead. Pilgrim roused himself, figured he'd cross before light fell. After one more drink and a few more words with the big man — who, in fact, beat him to it.

'Ain't you, Joe Pilgrim? I bin standin' here, looking, figurin'.'

'Yes, friend, that's my name.'

'You operated along the border?'

'Yeh, used to.'

'I come from down there. Joined my older brother, owns this place. But he's crippled with the rheumatics now so I came along to run things for him.'

'You saw me back there, huh?' Pilgrim wondered whether this big, tough-looking half-Siwash had belonged at one time to one of the border gangs.

'Saw you in EI Paso when you ran down the Salinas Kid. Think you were wearing a badge then.'

'Maybe. Can't remember.'

'You wearing a badge now, Mr Pilgrim?'

'Sort of.' Stretching a point a little. Now a chance for questions, which the big man listened to carefully. Then he said, 'They've been in here an' gone. Left town I guess.'

'They have. The old hostler told me that. Any trouble?'

'Not much you'd notice. On the edge. I heard one of the bunch call the handsome one who seemed to be the leader a name he didn't seem to like. Called him 'purty 'un'. But they drew in their horns, didn't want to draw too much attention to themselves likely. Got quiet again an' watchful. Then they left.'

'Purty 'un. That's a new one.' It was, Pilgrim thought. Who of the other three had thought that up? The odd one probably, the one not used to Michael Tagwell's leadership like his older pards Ripper and Dack were. The one called Benjy.

'An appropriate name did you think?'

'I guess. But the pretty one looked dangerous. A pushy sidewinder maybe more dangerous than the other three.'

'Likely.'

Pilgrim didn't stay much longer, took another drink, bought another for the barman, who called himself Jude, who said, 'Hope to see you again,' as the young manhunter, badge or no badge, took his leave.

5

They were on the other side of the river. The light was failing, and kind of ominous. There was no rain, though. Still and all, the humidity made the sweat pop from a man's skin.

They had been thinking of resting up a while but, on Michael's insistence, they plodded onwards, not knowing where he was leading, if any place special.

Their halt came suddenly, like a bombshell. Cal Ripper saw the snake, a black ribbon in the half-light. Ripper drew his gun but then couldn't see anything to shoot at.

The horse ridden by Ripper's pard Dack screamed and keeled over sideways.

Dack was thrown hard and one of the horse's hooves caught him on the side of the head, finishing the job.

Dack lay still. The rattler had disappeared, back to his clustered rocky hideaway.

Ripper holstered his gun. Michael said, nastily, 'Good job you didn't fire that thing. We don't know whether there's anybody behind us.'

'It's hardly likely I think,' Ripper said, figuring Michael didn't give a damn about Dack. But, hell, that was Michael all right! Ripper dismounted, got down on one knee beside Dack.

Neither Michael or Benjy dismounted. The latter said, 'That was a big 'un. Long an' fast like a stockwhip.'

'Had to be,' said Michael. 'Likely got the horse in the belly.'

Moaning, Dack began to squirm slightly, his senses returning. His face was running with blood from the damage to the side of his head. He hadn't gone to Eternity like his horse. But he looked pretty bad anyway.

Cal Ripper turned his head, looked back and up at the other two. 'He needs help right away.'

Michael said, 'Do the best you can for him.'

Michael's handsome features were set in a scowl. He was very disgruntled.

Ripper rose, got a spare clean bandanna from his saddle-bag, got down on his knee again. He worked quickly, feeling the other two's gaze on his back.

'We're short of a horse now,' said Michael.

Benjy didn't say anything. After their disagreement in the saloon on the other side of the river, the relations between the two men seemed to be on an even keel again, though they would never be completely so. Michael operated on vicious, murderous unpredictability, hardly seemed to know himself sometimes what exactly he was doing.

Ripper was quick, not gentle. Dack seemed to have passed out again with the pain. He had bitten his lip. Blood ran down his chin, so Ripper had some more wiping to do, using a dirty sweatcloth now. He had managed to bind the clean bandanna round Dack's head, though the blood was already soaking through it.

Ripper looked up again, said, 'Help me to get 'im up on the front of my horse.'

'Help him,' said Michael and, scowling, Benjy got down from his horse.

Benjy, the outsider, but Dack, too, was beginning to feel like the outsider now.

'Might as well shoot him,' said Benjy, as he joined Ripper and the unconscious man.

Ripper was half-turned, half-upright. He whirled on his heels, became upright, four-square. He was a tall, gangling man with a lean, ugly face and long arms. One of his arms came round like a whip and the fist at the end of it caught Benjy beautifully on the angle of his jaw.

Benjy was heavy, beetle-browed. He went over like a tree, his legs kicking like uprooted tendrils. He hit the ground hard, his eyes glazed. But he wasn't completely out. He was a tough brawler, noted for it.

It seemed he wasn't in the mood for fisticuffs now, and in the wrong position anyway. He reached for his gun.

Ripper's reaction was inevitable, but neither he nor Benjy was as fast as Michael. From the saddle, the handsome man had them both covered with his long-barrelled shooter.

'Put 'em back,' he said, 'or begod I'll blow you both away.'

They both let their half-drawn guns slide back into the holsters. 'It'll keep,' said Benjy. His square face looked a mite lopsided.

'Get him on the horse,' said Michael. Seemed he was on Dack's side now and the damaged hardcase seemed to appreciate this, eyes open as he moaned, cried out as he was bundled onto the front of Ripper's saddle.

'Let's get on,' said Michael. 'There's a settlement ahead.'

'I know,' said Benjy. It seemed he would say more. But he didn't.

Michael had carried the bank loot all along. They hadn't really had a chance for a share-out in quiet and comfort and away from prying eyes.

They gathered up Dack's warbag and assorted gear and Benjy took that. Michael said to leave the saddle, they hadn't room for it, throw it in the rocks. He didn't want anybody else to have it. They didn't argue with him, but Benjy said why not throw the dead horse in there, too? Michael gave him a hard, scornful look but made no further comment. With Dack clinging to the neck of Ripper's horse they at last set off, Michael leading the way ahead as if his tail was on fire.

The settlement that both he and Benjy seemed to know soon appeared ahead of them as a cluster of flickering lights in the darkness with black clouds scudding over a pale half-moon.

Ripper said he didn't think he'd seen the place before. Dack seemed to have passed out again. They got him to a doctor's surgery and the little bespectacled man said put him to bed, he'd fix him. The other three dumped Dack on a narrow cot and made for the nearest saloon, which was easy as it was the only one in the place, though there were hole-in-the-corner eating places in alleys; and booze dens, Benjy said. And the inevitable whorehouse and a few cribs, of course.

By now Michael was going through one of his high-falutin' secret phases and had little to say about the town or what or who he knew about it.

They left the horses at a livery stables. Michael toted the two saddlebags that held the loot. He gave no indication as to whether he'd want to stop long in this town.

The booze-den was fair-to-middlin' and not yet over-full. The three partners had mundane rye and equally mundane chow at a table in a quietish corner. They didn't talk much, but, over a desultory nothing it seemed, Benjy called Michael 'purty 'un' again.

'I told you not to call me that,'

Michael said, his pale, killer's eyes as icy as the tone of his voice.

The watching Ripper throught the big feller's spoiling for trouble — and he wondered why. He knew Benjy better than Michael did. Maybe Benjy didn't know Michael enough, didn't recognize that the handsome young man was more than a mite somewhat crazy.

Still, maybe Benjy was more than half that way himself. Ripper remembered how both Michael and Benjy had worked on old Dan Profett in the alley.

Cal Ripper had stayed look-out, telling himself that he was a gunfighter, not a bruiser. Anyway, he hadn't expected the old man to be killed.

Maybe Benjy had ideas of double-crossing Michael — and maybe Michael's partners, too, one of whom was pretty sick already. Ripper didn't know how his pard Dack was going to be. Maybe Benjy had some cocka-mamie plan about taking over from Michael. Who'd come out best? He decided he'd best watch both of them. But hell, he'd been doing that already, hadn't he? He hadn't the sadistic tendencies that the other two seemed to share, but he was tough, and he figured he'd be more than ready if anybody tried anything.

Benjy hadn't apologized for once more using the pet name he'd chosen for the boyish-looking Michael.

But Benjy was silent until a man came up to the table and greeted him by name in a mighty friendly fashion.

6

Pilgrim saw the vultures wheeling in the sky, black phantoms against the pale moon. He saw them plummeting past the dark clouds, appearing and disappearing like wraiths. But there was nothing ghostly about their peevish cries which rose intermittently in squabbling shrieks.

He smelled the dead horse before he came upon it. There was nothing else quite like the smell of a dead horse.

The vultures rose in a cloud, squabbling and protesting. They had done plenty of their gory work and Pilgrim didn't go near enough for a closer examination. He wondered whether this carcass, an unencumbered pile of bloody flesh, had belonged to one of the men he was following.

His own mount balked, shivered, although the night was hot, sticky. No matter how you looked at it, there was nasty unpleasantness in the air.

There was a rocky outcrop and Pilgrim left the horse and moved into this, the shadows, the slashes of moonlight like a fluctuating ghostly illumination. However, he spotted the saddle right away, wondered why it had been left. But maybe the riders hadn't had a place for it. Had a man been thrown from that illfated horse, been hurt, had to be carried, two men on one steed maybe?

He inspected the saddle as best he could, decided it was no great shakes. He left it, didn't find anything else.

Even if the small, bloody scene that he had come upon had been down to the four killers, he still didn't know how far he was behind them.

Maybe they had stayed overnight in the town which lay ahead of him. But by the time he got there it would be daylight and, even if they had sojourned there a while, they might be on their way again.

He had ridden hard.

From time to time, as the night went on, his pinto horse made snorting, disgruntled noises, tried a few jerky unco-ordinated movements, wasn't half as cheekily cheerful as he had been.

His rider called him names, but in gentle tones. He was an *amigo*, a prize. He quietened down, blew out his breath derisively as if he understood every word the man said — and maybe he did.

We're a couple of prize packages all right, Pilgrim thought. And the horse plodded steadily on.

But then the rain started again.

The driving, slashing storm-spots hit them head-on, cold, biting, refreshing after the humidity of the day and the evening. The horse for once seemed to welcome the downpour and plodded steadily, cheerfully now, the man thought. Knees going up and down. Hooves splashing and pumping.

Pilgrim knew he was still going in the right direction, but that was about all.

And even he began to doubt this when he saw the shape of the house ahead, lone on the prairie.

He didn't remember a house being around there and this certainly wasn't the outskirts of town.

Getting nearer, he began to figure that the main structure and the outhouses and corral were pretty new. There was a veranda. No lights shone. But then, as the wet and weary traveller reined in the horse, a yellow glow blossomed in the lower floor of the stout, two-storey building. Then the front door opened and a tall figure came out on the veranda and Pilgrim saw the gleam of a shotgun barrel and a deep voice called, 'Stay right where you're at, stranger.'

★   ★   ★

Michael carried his appendage wherever he went, like a man with a hump. A golden hump. And his two pards stayed close to him and his hump, for the hump was golden for them also and they didn't trust mercurial Michael: not even the handsome man's long-time pard Ripper wholly trusted him now.

Michael wanted to see how the damaged Dack was getting along, so he left the saloon and Benjy and Ripper tailed at his heels. Benjy had said he knew some fine gals at the whorehouse, but Michael said he wasn't in the mood for that now. Not yet anyway . . .

Ripper had said he didn't care one way or the other. Actually, he was somewhat anxious about Dack, though he didn't tell the other two about these feelings. He was surprised that Michael also seemed worried about him. Maybe the pretty man had a heart after all. Or he was suffering from one of his rare sunny moods?

Come to think of it, there was nothing sunny about the weather now, black dark and all: the rain was coming down in sheets when, after dodging from shelter to shelter, they finally reached the doctor's surgery. Hell, there hadn't been any wet at all when they left the saloon and Benjy grumbled that he wished he'd stayed there.

Ripper didn't believe a word of that. Benjy wasn't aiming to take his peepers off those bulging saddle-bags!

The sudden rain hadn't awakened the elderly doctor who was as peevish as a fighting cock that had actually gotten its feathers wet.

Michael apologized very politely, said they hadn't realized how late it was, the saloon still being open and all.

The doc said that that saloon was open every damn' night, all night, although the good folk of the town had been trying to get it to shut at some reasonable hour.

The three visitors figured that this was a wide open town anyway with no law to speak of and a so-called mayor (Benjy said) who was too fat to lace up his own boots. This was a sort of calling-in hidey-hole for such venal drifters and their sick friend Dack.

The doc wore only a robe and

slippers. 'Go in and see him then for godsakes,' he said, didn't offer to accompany them.

Saddle-bags draped over his back, Michael made a bee-line for the slightly open door behind which Dack lay. Benjy followed close on his heels. Ripper decided he'd like to see Dack on his own, talk to him if that was possible. They'd been together off and on for a long time. Since they were tads in fact. Besides, he wanted to check with this old fart, dithering and moping in his robe and slippers. What kind of a sawbones was he anyway?

'How's he gonna be?'

'You close to him?' The old man had his specs over his rheumy eyes now and peered at Ripper like an owl.

'He's my cousin.' Likely; though the ramifications of their respective families had been as convoluted as nasty, stinking, creepy ivy and as poisonous sometimes.

'I think he's going to be all right,' said the doc, almost benign now.

7

'So you're Marshal Joe's son,' said the big man with the iron-grey hair as he leaned his shotgun against the wall.

'That's what I am all right, suh,' said young Joe Pilgrim.

'When I first built up this place I bought some stock from your dad. Is he still goin' strong?'

'Yeh. Him and the ranch.'

'And that lovely sister of yours Rebbie, and her tall husband. I disremember his name. I know he's a fine ramrod.'

'Cal's his name. Yes, suh, they're doing fine.'

The big man, whose name was Pete Teller, had already told Pilgrim that he was wary of strangers because there'd been trouble lately. With rustlers. Or night riders who behaved like rustlers. Pete hadn't amplified the last somewhat ambiguous remark.

But Pete had added also that he was alone here with his daughter at night (their two hands bunked in town) since his wife had died a couple of years ago. Just after they built the place on this land in fact. A sad story.

The girl came into the room. Dressed in a long maroon-coloured robe that didn't hide her slim figure, she was sleepy-eyed, with tousled, dark-gold hair. Pilgrim thought she looked mighty delectable. Pete introduced her as his daughter Arabella. She said she'd met Mr Pilgrim's father, a nice man. Her hand-clasp was warm and firm. Her eyes, brightening, were of a limpid green.

'I'll make coffee,' she said, and moved through a door that obviously led to a kitchen.

Pilgrim asked her father, 'What about this trouble you mentioned?' This young man wasn't the sort to be given to procrastination. He shot plumb from the hip.

Pete said, 'A few riders. Never got a shot at 'em. Hardly glimpsed 'em. Heard 'em. They roused the cattle, but, strangely, didn't steal but three all told, though they visited here a couple o' times and we've heard strange noises in the night since then. We managed to round up the beef. 'Cept the three — and they might have wandered off further, we thought o' that. Strange, huh?'

'Yeh. Sounds like a kind of harass-ment.'

'Hope it don't get worse then,' said Pete. 'I did hear a rumour that a big ranching combine, damn' dudes 'tis said, are aiming to get as much o' these valley lands as they can.'

Nothing more was said then as Arabella came back with the coffee. I'm after four killers and I must find them, Pilgrim thought, but what else have I sort of run into now?

Marshal Joe would have wanted to know . . .

* * *

Benjy stood by the door which he'd closed behind him. Michael walked over to the sleeping man in the bed.

Dack looked peaceful, breathing gently.

Michael turned his head. 'See that door is closed tightly,' he said.

'It is.'

Michael bent over the bed, over the still form.

Benjy waited, leaning against the door.

* * *

Michael turned, made for the door.

Opening the door, Benjy preceded him into the other room.

Cal Ripper and the doc turned their heads. Then Michael's manner changed dramatically.

'Goddammit, you didn't look after him properly. He's had a seizure or something. Damn your soul, the man is

52

dead — he's dead.'

Ripper pushed past Michael and Benjy and went through into the bedroom. He was soon back, said, 'Dack is dead all right.'

The doc began, 'I can assure you gentlemen that . . . '

Michael cut in on him. 'Well, I suppose there's nothing we can do about it now. Dead is dead.' Another complete change of demeanour.

Death was no new thing to any of these people. Ripper said quietly, 'We'll have to see him funeraled.'

'We'll see about that.' Michael looked hard at the little doctor. 'For the meantime we'll leave him where he is. You hear me, old man?'

'I hear you.' The little man looked tired to death himself but, as the three men left, he was making his way into the bedroom.

'We can't risk staying here and seeing Dack buried,' said Michael, as they made their way automatically back to the saloon.

Nobody argued with that logic. 'I'm gonna find an undertaker, though,' said Ripper. 'I'm gonna pay him to see that Dack is buried properly.'

'Be quick about it then,' said Michael. 'I want to leave here soon.' He made no mention of the friend he had said earlier that he had in this town.

Benjy hadn't actually introduced the friend he had here either, but the feller turned up in the saloon again and approached the two men at the corner table. By that time Ripper had gone in search of an undertaker, though he might have to wake that individual up from his beauty sleep. Ripper, who was nothing but forthright, would manage to do that all right.

Benjy's friend greeted him as if they were kissin' cousins. He brought them both a drink. Michael eyed him warily and then decided to put on the charm.

The charm worked on Benjy's friend, who was named Carl. He wasn't blocky like Benjy but lean — fast with his movements but not with his brain. With cards, with knives and pretty good with a shooter also.

Michael said he had to go out to the privy. Benjy watched him go out through the side door then followed him, leaving Carl at the table.

Benjy returned quickly, not wanting to be spotted by Michael, though Benjy didn't trust the man one atom. And Michael, of course, had toted the golden saddle-bags to the privy with him. Michael returned, all smiles. But before that handsome visage had put in an appearance again, Benjy had had a chance to have a few swift and pregnant words with his old friend Carl.

The two conspirators were now all smiles also. That fancy-pants with the fancy jib thought he was hell on wheels! But more than one could play at that game.

Just then Ripper returned, said he'd fixed things with the local undertaker, had paid him some cash on the barrel. The doleful gent would see that Dack had a proper funeral come morning, with a hearse and black horses and a proper preacher and even a few mourners who would undertake such a chore for a fair cash consideration, one an old female body who could wail like a banshee.

Neither of Dack's erstwhile partners offered to share funeral expenses with Dack's 'cousin' Ripper, but they did allow Carl to buy the man a drink.

Maybe newcomer Carl figured to get some come-back later.

8

Carl said that the girls down at the local cathouse were throwing some kind of a circus tonight, for favoured guests only. And Carl himself was one of those.

He said he'd be honoured if his old friend Benjy and Benjy's two friends would join him. 'Not a big place, gentlemen,' he said. 'And no questions asked. The best little whorehouse in the territory.'

'It is purty good as I remember,' said Benjy, with a sideways look at Michael.

'I ain't in the mood,' Michael said, which was the second time he'd said something like that tonight.

'I'll go ahead then,' said Carl, somewhat miffed it seemed, and he rose and they lost sight of him.

'We could sleep there,' said Benjy. 'It'd be a fine hideout. At the end o' town, an' nobody taking notice of us if we leave in the early morning.'

'He's got a point there, Michael,' said Ripper.

'Maybe later,' said the handsome man.

And later, magnanimously, he rose with a sort of flourish and said, 'Let's go then' and led the way.

The back way.

Carl had thought that his put-out hadn't worked, but he'd stayed in the alley anyway. He had, however, been about to move when the back door of the booze-den opened, releasing a shaft of yellow light which illuminated Michael as he stepped on to the hard sod.

Carl had expected Benjy to lead the way, if Michael changed his mind that is. Benjy had said that the fancy-pants was a mighty changeable sort of gent. It seemed Michael had changed his mind this night — and then some!

He marched out into the dark alley like he hadn't a thought in his handsome head except a young whore cutting a caper. Hurrying towards it. And Carl there with his trusty bowie already in his hand.

But Carl had kind of misjudged Michael. As many had done before him.

★   ★   ★

It was late but they were still talking. They had taken more coffee, this time laced with rye whiskey. Arabella took her part. What a wonderful throat she has, Pilgrim thought, and her green eyes mocked him as if she'd read his mind.

There was no coquetry in her at all, though, just a hospitable and warm friendliness.

The night was quiet except for their voices. The three of them spoke of many things. They talked about ranching, about the Tellers' small spread and about Marshal Joe's larger place on the other side of the Pecos, a much bigger spread now than it had been, and still growing, though young Joe said he wanted no part of it yet. Still and all, his father, retired famous lawman, had had his problems in the early days.

In those early days, Joe had helped a lot but had fiddlefooted widely also. Only recently had he figured he might go back for a longer spell, maybe even settle. But he did not talk of that now.

It was only when Arabella rose and wandered over to the window, its curtains wide in the hospitable way and the lamplight streaming out, that there was a lull in the talking. And a subtle change.

The girl said, 'I thought I heard something out there. I can't see anything.'

As one, her father and the younger man joined her.

Out there in the night and beyond the spread of yellow light the flames blossomed suddenly, like an explosion.

'The barn,' Pete Teller said, and he ran for the door, Pilgrim close on his heels.

'Watch yourselves,' the girl called.

The two men, alarmed, quick but not stupid, acted like staunch frontier fighters. Pilgrim, in his passage, yanked his gun rig from the back of a chair. Pete lifted his elderly, formidable Sharps rifle from behind the door.

He yelled back at the girl, 'Stay where you are, honey. Put out the lamp.'

The light went out. The girl was capable, unafraid. The men's motion was a crouching one as they went through the door, fanned out, one at each side. They could hear the flames now but nothing else. They half-circled into the shadows.

'Hooves,' Pilgrim called from his shadowland. And from his partial cover too, Pete made a gesture to signal that he had heard the hoofbeats too, drumming, fading.

★ ★ ★

The pall of smoke in the cathouse was getting so bad that it was difficult for anybody, unless they were right near, to make out the gyrations of the girls and their partners of both kinds. The view was intermittently titillating but hardly ideal.

The two cowboys, called Pink and Seal respectively, were neither of them tall men. Mere striplings, they'd been lucky to be allowed around this shindig in the first place. But Big Lucky who, compared to the other girls, was kind of long in the tooth — and fat to boot — had taken a fancy to Seal, who looked as if he needed mothering, and had let him and his pard through a back door.

The two cowhands now used the same door to get out and, as the cooler air hit them, Pink said, 'That damn' place makes me cough.'

Seal giggled. 'Big Lucky would make anybody cough,' he said.

'Hell, you ain't really been with her,' snorted Pink, and the snort turned into a phlegmy rattle.

'Hey!' said Seal, digging his partner in the ribs with an elbow.

'Sufferin' hell,' expostulated Pink. 'Will you quit it.'

But now Seal was pointing a forefinger.

Way out there was a red glow in the sky.

Pink stopped wheezing, stuck his head forward, said, 'That's in our area.'

'Sure is. Could be the place.'

'Do you reckon we ought to go see?'

'I reckon,' said Seal. The lightweight of the pair he was already moving towards where they'd stashed their horses.

★   ★   ★

Michael had the twin saddle-bags which contained the precious haul over his right shoulder. As wary as a wildcat, as Ripper, Benjy and he moved out of the saloon into the alley he had taken his gun out of its holster, concealing it by the bags.

Michael didn't like Benjy's friend Carl, didn't trust him, didn't trust

63

Benjy either, in truth didn't trust anybody.

When Carl came at him with the wicked-looking, broad-bladed knife, Michael shot from the hip, the muzzle of his gun tilted upwards. He couldn't miss. Carl went backwards as if he'd been kicked under the chin. His head hit the hard sod and his legs kicked up.

Michael whirled on Benjy who exclaimed 'Hey' in complete shocked surprise. Ripper was bringing up the rear. He knew Michael better than Benjy did and certainly better than the late living Carl had. But even Ripper was taken by surprise.

Benjy tried to grab Michael's gun-hand and in so doing knocked the saddle-bags from the man's shoulder. Michael triggered his gun once more and Benjy took the slug in the belly and cried out inarticulately and crumpled.

Michael bent and picked up the saddle-bags, glancing upwards and sideways at Ripper as he did so, saying, 'Those shots will have been heard. We don't need any complications. Let's get out of here.'

*   *   *

They ran a chain of buckets and the girl helped. Tacit agreement between Pilgrim and Pete was that it would be useless to chase the miscreants who'd set the fire as they had too big a start.

The horses were milling in the corral which was adjacent to the burning barn which was already beginning to fall in upon itself, couldn't be saved. Arabella took it upon herself to gentle the horses as the men damped down the dying fire, the structure that was turning into a mere pile of smouldering rubbish.

'Harassment,' stormed Pete. 'Pure harassment.' His voice sank to a whisper. 'Those bastards. *Those bastards!*'

'Somebody else is comin',' Pilgrim said. Then he was out on the sod, gun in hand. And a voice called out.

'It's my two boys,' yelled Pete. 'They

must've spotted the glow. It's Pink an' Seal.'

Seal was still yelling as the two boys reined in. 'Did you see anybody?' Pete demanded.

Seal shut up. It was Pink who gave his boss the answer. 'We didn't see a soul, but we heard hoofbeats off in the distance. Not going towards town but way out.'

'They did what they had to do,' said Pete, his voice lowering again. 'They won't be back tonight.'

The two cowboys dismounted and began to give a hand.

Part Two

Blood-Tracks

9

Leaving the little spread and Arabella and Pete and the two boys was, for a time, like pulling his own teeth, Pilgrim thought. He knew that in particular he would miss Arabella, even after such a short acquaintance and, strangely, this knowledge he accepted without surprise.

Already folks were moving from other spreads, none of them greatly large, to help the Tellers in their clean-up. Nobody else had been harassed on the same night but there had been, as Pete Teller had told Pilgrim, similar incidents at other times, both at his spread and at others.

This was the first time, however, that the mysterious night riders' depredations had stretched to barn-burning.

In the early morning, Pilgrim reached the town and rode into new troubles.

Two men had been shot in an alley. One was dead, the other fighting for his life. The latter person was the hardcase Pilgrim had known, though not intimately, as Benjy. And Benjy was one of the three men Pilgrim had been tracking after the killings and the bank robbery back home.

Benjy was in bed in back of the local sawbones' place and Pilgrim went to see him there. The doc didn't know whether the man was going to make it. The patient didn't know it either, and neither did his visitor. But Benjy was ready to talk to a man he knew by sight and reputation, a man bent on retribution. And Benjy wanted part of that now — *vengeance*.

He talked in halting, agonized tones and Pilgrim had to give him time. Pilgrim had patience now and an implacable resolve. Benjy lay in the bed where his erstwhile partner Dack had died and the quiet, poker-faced, young gunfighter on an upright deal chair, listened.

The death of Dack. Murdered by Michael. But Dack's bosom friend, cousin maybe, Ripper, hadn't known about that, had accepted Dack's death as an unfortunate tragedy. And Ripper was on the trail again with Michael.

'I figure Michael's planning to double-cross Ripper too,' Benjy said. He had not actually admitted that he and his town friend, Carl, had themselves tried a double-cross. Pilgrim had had to figure that for himself: it hadn't been hard.

'I'll tell you somep'n else that might be useful,' Benjy went on. But then he had to lie back in the bed, gasping, while Pilgrim waited, watching him with expressionless dark eyes which seemed to bore into him, cajoling, *forcing.*

'Michael had a friend in town and Carl told me who. But I don't think Michael had time to get in touch with this friend ... ' Benjy was gasping again.

'Tell me who,' Pilgrim cajoled.

'A rich old Mexican from a big ranchero over the border. He has holdings of some sort here, too; a rich, powerful old don. I reckon Michael wants to settle in Mexico where the American law can't get at him . . . '

'The name?'

'Don Esteban Monaro. I — I don't rightly know whether he's still here or where he hangs out when he is. He's a secretive ol' cuss . . . ' Strangely, Benjy began to laugh. But this turned to a cough; then a gasping fight for breath.

'I'll find him,' said Pilgrim half to himself.

He called the doc.

★ ★ ★

'Don Esteban left town very early this morning, *señor*,' the little Mexican said. 'My country — and his — eet is far away.'

'I guess it is at that,' said Pilgrim laconically. He had an idea that he wasn't going to get much out of this

72

sloe-eyed cuss. But he tried. 'Heard that the old don stayed here, in this place.'

He thought he saw a flicker of surprise in the dark eyes. But it disappeared. 'He ees my oncle, *señor*.'

Well, that explained something anyway. Pilgrim had tried first of all the so-called hotel. A mere clapboard lodging-house, but the best place in town to put up in somebody had said. Travellers didn't seem to stay long in this town anyway. 'Wide open' it might be, but it wasn't exactly salubrious.

A remark from a kid at the livery stables had led Pilgrim to this tumble-down dump on the edge of town. Hardly the kind of place where a don would stay — unless to keep company with a relative, of course, and the average don was supposed to look out for his family, wasn't he? Unless a member broke a blood oath or something . . .

Oh, but there were a lot of good Mexes: Pilgrim had known some mighty fine ones. They weren't all renegades or *bandidos* as many Norte-Americanos were wont to think. The little man who stood before Pilgrim now was a loyal member of his clan. He wouldn't tell this Anglo, this smooth-talking *gringo*, where exactly Don Esteban Monaro might be going.

The badly wounded Benjy hadn't known all that much after all. Pilgrim wondered fleetingly how Benjy was faring. But then he left the end of town and went back to the doc's place, only to learn that Benjy had handed in his pail and had joined the shell of his old friend, Dack, down at the undertaking parlour.

Pilgrim had already learned that there was no kind of law here, although there was an old drunk ex-lawyer who called himself mayor. Right now, though, the personage would be sleeping the sleep of the deep in the still-early morning.

Two men had died. Hardcases. Saddletramps. Their kind had died in this town before and no doubt more would in the future. You could stake a prime hand on that, Pilgrim figured. The place had a mighty bad rep.

Pete Teller had said that the town didn't bother them, however, that he didn't think who'd been raising hell out on the range had anything to do with the town but had come from much further afield.

Rustling would be too much like hard work for the types who sojourned in or passed through the town. Not that there had been any actual rustling, not that you could *call* out-and-out cattle or horse stealing, nothing like that could be proven. That was a strange but maybe significant fact.

As far as Pilgrim knew nobody had gone after the shooters from the alley by the saloon. Nobody in the saloon seemed to have seen anything, wouldn't have attached any importance to it if they had, likely. Not unless it was aimed at them, which it wasn't. No down-and-out private, falling-out killing should be allowed to interfere with the serious business of drinking, gambling, dallying with the girls and whispered parleying about nefarious schemes.

These weren't clever people or they wouldn't have elected to bide in this hell-hole in the first place.

Pilgrim visited again the livery stables where he'd gotten dubious information from the kid. The kid's boss, an inveterate boozer who seldom rose early, had arrived now. The kid was his nephew and stayed in the same boarding-house, was awakened by his uncle in the early morning and sent down to his early duties before the old soak got his head down again.

From his window, the old man had spotted the two strangers leaving town on their horses. The old coot said to Pilgrim now, 'I don't lock the place up like a damn' fortress. One thing folks don't do in this town is steal horses. That ain't the thing at all unless you want your neck stretched to Kingdom Come. Them fellers must've got them beasts out by themselves . . . '

'I didn't see 'em,' put in the kid, 'not this mawnin'. But I did see 'em when they came in. The fancy-pants, I well remember him. I liked the look of his duds.' The kid's own duds were veritable rags. 'There were four of 'em then,' the kid said. 'One of 'em wasn't ridin' well.'

'They did that shootin' I guess,' said the old man. 'Then they hid out a bit before leaving town. Likely. Though it was still kinda dark when I see'd 'em.'

'Which way did they go?' Pilgrim asked.

The old man told him.

10

Pilgrim decided that he had to think of places where Michael and Ripper would hole up again, if only for a short spell. Holes in corners, soddie settlements and camps of travellers who moved around a lot. Tents, hills, rock outcrops, canyons, drywater beds, ghost towns: the strange places that were a part of this sprawling, lawless, legendary area of the great South-west.

The trail Pilgrim followed was a well-worn, ancient one, a throwback to the old days and, as such, a lonely trail also.

The man had not seen man nor beast for some time since passing a few cowboys with a small herd of cattle going in the opposite direction to him, the men waving to the lone rider companionably from a distance.

The light was beginning to fall below

a sinking red sun. The rider talked to his horse, to himself, not making a whole lot of sense. Then they both saw the cluster of shacks ahead of them and the horse quickened his pace as if he smelled welcome sustenance.

Of a sudden, Pilgrim remembered the place, knew where he was. In the old days this had been a stagecoach road. The cluster of shacks had been the stage stop before a rail spur had been built a few miles away and the 'iron horse' had taken over.

There was still plenty of room at the station. The buildings didn't look too dilapidated, were even welcoming, warm-looking under the dying sun, wisps of pale smoke rising from somewhere in the middle there.

Pilgrim led his horse through out-houses where there were no signs of life, whether animal or human. He came to the main place, the house, and there was an open door and through that a figure appeared, a revolver in each hand like a gunslinger on the prod.

Pants, riding boots, scraggy black hair, appearing youthful until the voice rang out.

'Hold it there, stranger, or I'll blow you right outa the saddle.'

A husky but undeniably feminine voice.

Pilgrim reined in, said, 'I come in peace. I'm looking for two men. A handsome young fancy-pants and his scruffy, not-so-handsome sidekick who is somewhat older.'

'The've been here. They hurt my dad. One of 'em did anyways. He's back in the house. You a lawman, mister?'

'Sort of.' Pilgrim raised his empty hands shoulder-high. 'I guess I might be able to help your dad.' He jerked his head sideways, indicating a small outhouse a few yards away. 'Look, I'll stash my hardware over there.'

He eased the horse over. The muzzles of the girl's two guns didn't waver. He got down slowly from the horse, keeping well into the girl's sight as he did so. He carefully took his Winchester from its saddle scabbard and leaned it against the wall.

He unbuckled his gun belt with one hand, bending a mite but still looking straight at the girl. He let the hardware fall to the sod with a dull thud and with the toe of his boot eased it over to join the rifle.

He approached the girl and she let him pass and precede her through the main door. Following him, she let her guns dangle at her side.

The elderly man lay in bed in the largest of the two rooms in back of the single-storey building. His head was bandaged but he was blearily awake and demanded, 'What's goin' on?'

'My name's Pilgrim, suh,' said the young visitor quickly before the two-gun girl could speak. 'It appears you've already met the two men I'm trailin'.'

'I met 'em all right. One of 'em pistol-whipped me. You a lawman?'

Pilgrim gave the father the same answer he'd given the daughter. And, like her, he seemed satisfied with that, and went on, 'My girl fixed my head. But I'm having trouble with my shoulder. It feels as if it's busted.'

'Can I take a look?'

'Surely.' The man seemed to have accepted the visitor and, looking past him as he bent forward, said to the girl. 'Put them guns away, honey. It's all right.'

'Yes, Pa.' There was a small clatter as she put the two pistols on a nearby table.

Pilgrim pulled back the bedclothes. The injured man still wore his checked shirt and tried to unbutton it with his left hand, wincing. It was obviously his right shoulder that was damaged.

'I'll do that,' said Pilgrim and the man let him, lined face beaded with sweat, eyes flickering with pain.

'It's dislocated,' Pilgrim said.

'I fell on it.'

'Yeh, that'd do it. There doesn't seem

to be any actual broken bones, so I think I can fix it. If you'll take a chance with me that is.'

'I will.'

'You a drinkin' man, suh?' Pilgrim asked.

'He is,' said the daughter sharply. She had moved to the other side of the bed and Pilgrim raised his head and looked straight at her, the first time he'd done this. Two guns in the hand of a determined female who might or not be some kind of shooting fool was hardly a situation to prove conducive to exhaustive inspection.

She wasn't bad to look at. Her hair was cropped short and not too well which, with the work pants she wore was what had first made the visitor take her to be a boy. The hair was as black as a raven's wing and topped a face which was ruddily chubby and pleasant, sort of cheerful-looking, roguish even.

Her figure was plumpish too, and very curvaceous, her breasts thrusting ripely against her grimy, once-white linsey blouse.

She gave him what might be called a roguish look from big, bluey-grey eyes and, when he asked, 'Have you got any hooch?', the glance became almost mischievous and, without answering, she turned away and moved to the door, her buttocks moving with a delectable rhythm in the tight pants. She had even left her two guns behind.

She soon returned, a bottle in each hand, a far more friendly sight than the twin guns reposing on the table side by side. They were obviously her father's weapons and workmanlike and well-kept, a pair of heavy Colt Dragoons. Pilgrim was mighty glad that he hadn't made any quick moves out there on the sod under the dying sun.

'Take a slug yourself,' she said and he did this. Then he turned to the man in the bed and gave him one of the bottles.

'Take all you can.'

That was plenty. The man in the bed was a seasoned toper and had a mighty good excuse now. He made the most of it, and soon he was out, his chin wet. Well out.

Pilgrim got to work and the girl watched, though he'd told her she needn't if she didn't want to: he wouldn't yet need any help. In his leanness he was a strong, muscular man. The watching girl winced and made small exclamations but didn't interfere, obviously admiring the expertise of this dangerous-looking, capable young stranger who called himself Pilgrim.

Only at the end did the older man begin to moan, and Pilgrim gave him more whiskey, looked at the girl again. 'I'll need some more strong bandaging to finish the job.'

'I'll get some.'

He couldn't help but watch her go, admiring the way she moved. She didn't seem to have been harmed by those two outlaws. He had questions to ask. But they would keep a while longer.

11

Although the Teller place hadn't been hit again, strange incidents had taken place in other parts of the territory. Another barn burning for instance. The Tellers, Pete and Arabella had a new barn, erected with the help of neighbours and the two cowboys, Pink and Seal.

Those two usually bunked in town as there wasn't quite enough room at the small ranch. Maybe they preferred to be away from work on their off-times anyway.

Now, with the way things were, they elected to stay at the ranch. In fact, they took up abode in the new barn, turned it into a dandy sleeping place for themselves.

There was little doubt that they were mighty fond of Pete and his daughter, particularly the latter, whom, in the

Western way, they treated with the utmost courtesy, addressing her as Miss Arabella at all times.

During this period nothing untoward happened in town, rough though the place was, but news came from other places not too far afield. Cattle stampeded, but it seemed not a single beef was actually stolen and all were gathered finally, except for one that maybe somebody kept for a souvenir. Folks became strangely suspicious of their neighbours, which was maybe just what the night riders aimed them to be. Uneasy feelings prevailed.

Shooting in the night but no casualties, except a quarrelsome hound dog, dead, but with bloody jaws. It was figured that the hound had bitten his killer; but no dog-bitten personage was heard of in any place.

Two cowboys riding home late from town were surrounded by masked riders (later one admitted that there'd only been four of 'em, but they'd had the drop all right) and had been whipped from horseback, their steeds sent galloping on, had been forced to walk, weals and all.

Fences had been roped and dragged, wires cut, windows smashed. Two men caught wandering on a neighbour's land had been beaten up by a bunch of the neighbour's hands. A range war was feared. Bad feelings bubbled under the surface. But then there was a welcome lull. *Until* . . .

News travelled in the early morning of a killing at the biggest ranch in the territory, the one furthest from the town. A rider shot in the back of the head as he rode with the dogies. No news of masked riders on that night, however. And the evil, hidden brew was fermenting again: rumour, innuendo, hard words, suspicions, shouted arguments and useless speculations, neighbour against neighbour, cowhand against townie. Strangers were watched. But strangers came and went, always had in this lawless territory. Nobody could keep tabs. As for the regular townies: they had seldom been known to shit too near their own nests.

Pete Teller said to his daughter, 'I want you to go and stay in town . . . '

'I'm all right here,' Arabella put in. 'I want to stay with you and the boys.'

'I want you to go and stay with Elga.'

Elga was a cousin of Pete's who ran a millinery business and was liked and respected by all, was sassy and outspoken and unafraid of man nor beast.

'I know I'd be all right with Elga. But I don't want to stay in town. If you're thinking of more trouble happening hereabouts . . . ' She snorted in exasperation. 'Jeepers, I can shoot straighter than you or any one of the boys, and you know it. They know it, too, I guess.'

That was a fact all right! Pete was speechless. Arabella loved shooting. Though as far as he knew she had never shot anything bigger than a rabbit, she was a dandy cracksman on bottles and cans. She had shooting contests with the boys, mostly with her rifle. Maybe

Pink was better with a handgun, but that was all. And Seal was kind of hamfisted, though the best cowhand and horseman of the two.

Pete knew that he was beaten. Come hell or high water Arabella aimed to stay here. He'd have to make sure that one or other of the boys was on watch for her all the time, when he, Pete, was absent, like at the cowmen's meeting that was to take place soon at the big ranch where the hand had been killed, and nobody yet indicted for it.

There would doubtless be jostlings between Pink and Seal to determine who would be Arabella's bodyguard at any given time. Arabella would be able to handle that all right, though, Pete was sure of it. Hell, she could wrap both of 'em around her little finger, no trouble at all.

★   ★   ★

The damaged elderly man who lived with his daughter in the disused stage station was called Bill Daylas. His roguish daughter was Delia.

A widower for some years, he had left Wells Fargo and moved to the nearby small town of Daliento and taken on a general stores. But he'd had competition. Then he had a bright idea. He approached Wells Fargo with a proposal. He took over the station that had once been his home, his work, and began to do his business from there.

At first he did very well, for the old trail was still popular. Then the rail spur was built in back of Daliento and business dwindled. Bill still kept stuff around, however, and did odd jobs both at home and back in town (he had no ambition to actually move back there) and things sort of scraped along. Delia was a good cook and cleaner, Bill told his visitor, the elderly cuss grinning lopsided with his bruised face.

Pilgrim was back in territory he had visited before and he remembered Daliento, a bustling little place no better, no worse, than many of its somewhat lawless neighbours. There was a string of such settlements between here and the border in spots where the badlands didn't encroach.

He wondered what plump Delia thought of being stuck out here in the near-wilds instead of in town, young girl like her alone with her old man except when visitors called, buyers sometimes, but also saddletramps. And hardcases like the two who'd come last, before the lean, poker-faced shrewd-eyed young man called Pilgrim.

Pilgrim didn't ask intimate questions about man or girl, let the former ramble on. A potted biography, and another story told with indignation.

*　*　*

Delia had left the room. It had been evident from meaningful sidelong glances that her father wanted her to do this.

Sitting up in bed with his arm in a sling, his one undamaged eye fixed on

Pilgrim (the other was blackened and closed) Bill Daylas said, 'I did my best. But that pup was too much for me. Only him, only one of 'em. Had I been younger, begod . . . But that pup knew all the tricks an' all.'

'Which one?'

'The fancy one, not the other one. Y'see, he tried tricks with Delia an' I went for him. He took his gun to me. I went down hard. I must've lost my senses. Them boys rode off. Delia said the ugly one wanted to get goin', pronto.'

'Did they take anything?'

'A few supplies. Which is what they'd wanted in the first place. They didn't steal anything. They left cash on the barrelhead. More'n was necessary. Like — one or the other — was sort of apologizing for the way they'd treated Delia. One of 'em anyway. Me an' Delia. Goddamn fancy-boots acted like he hadn't had a woman for a helluva long time. Still an' all, I figured he'd have killed the both of us if he'd had a mind to.'

That was right, Pilgrim thought, as a while later he rode on his way.

Had plump, curvaceous Delia's roguish glances precipitated Michael Tagwell's behaviour towards her?

He chided himself for thinking ill of the girl who had given him a bright welcome.

Nah, he hadn't really meant it!

But Delia had certainly had a way with her, and now the cogitating horse-rider couldn't help contrasting her with Arabella who he thought, he *hoped*, was waiting for him back there in the Pecos territory.

Women were complicated. Oh, yes. But, Arabella, there was a straight one! More beautiful than Delia also — no roguish coquetry there.

Maybe Delia just couldn't help herself. Like Michael Tagwell couldn't help himself.

A killer acting a part. But still a soulless murderer with no heart and no conscience. There but for the grace . . .

A sobering thought.

Did the man know that, if only indirectly, he had been responsible for the death of his own father, a respected banker and a loving man, a straight man. Had he known, would he care?

How could you fathom a thing like Michael Tagwell? How could you judge such a man? He'd had a good life with parents who had doted on him. He had worked at the bank only when he felt like it, although he had had a good schooling, had been supposed to have a good business head. He was no Indian fighting for his very existence, no *peon* scrabbling for enough *dinero* to keep body and soul together, no slum-kid or soddie-dweller living on scraps.

The solution: a hang-rope or a bullet in the head. That was it! But, a sudden weariness overtaking him, Pilgrim realized that the prospect of a hemp or hot-lead sacrifice for such scum as fancy Michael did not please his soul as much as it would have done in his younger, *roaring* days.

12

He had, of course, asked about Don Esteban Monaro and Bill Daylas had surprised him.

Monaro had passed by the station-cum-stores on horseback not so long after the 'purty 'un' and his sidekick had left. Pilgrim might have figured that. But it was the second part that had surprised him.

Bill Daylas had known Monaro well in, as he put it, 'the old days'. Now the Mexican man claimed to be of fine Spanish blood. But he was in fact a *mestizo*, Bill said — or mostly. His grandfather had been an Apache brave who had taken a Mexican girl captive, as 'wife'. She had borne him one son and then had died during a fever epidemic that had decimated the tribe.

The boy, though, had lived, had grown strong, had taken a Mexican bride and started a ranch mainly with stolen Norte-Americano cattle. He had had a daughter, and then a son. His wife had died and, like many of his kind, the husband had given up his ranch and taken to the owlhoot trail.

His daughter had run away, had become a high-priced *puta* in Santa Fe. The boy, who was called Pedro, had gone with his father and, while still young, had taken over leadership of the gang after his old man had been killed in a gun battle with *rurales* beyond the border.

'They were a bunch of soulless *comancheros*,' Bill said. And Pilgrim had wondered just how well the old stageline man and storekeeper had known such people when he was young and wild and full of piss and vinegar. But that was not Pilgrim's business.

The one called Pedro had been the most ruthless, amoral and clever of all those in the border gang and he had prospered and made himself a new life with a big Mexican ranch and a new name, Don Esteban. But at heart, Bill Daylas affirmed, he was still the devil from Hell that he'd always been.

'He rode past here without a glance in this direction. Upright on a fine horse and, to him now, us like *peons* at the roadside. He always rode well upright in his high-backed Mexican saddle, always with changes of horses on his trail. I figure he'll pick up a new mount in Daliento this time. It would soon be arranged for the great Don Esteban Monaro.'

So it was to Daliento that Joe Pilgrim was now making his way. And would Monaro pick up something else in that town besides a horse? Would he meet an ally there and, if so, why?

And who?

★ ★ ★

Ripper had called him 'purty 'un', in front of that girl and her father too. Benjy had used to call him that. But Benjy was dead now. And so was Dack.

And Benjy's friend Carl (or whatever his name was) had been laid low.

Michael had killed both Dack and Benjy, hoped what's-his-name, Benjy's pard, had also handed in his pail by now.

Ripper didn't know just how his bosom friend Dack had come about his death at the hands of Michael. It would have been more than a mite awkward if he had.

Four men with boodle to split four ways, with Michael, the leader, getting the largest share. Now there was only two of them and, at first, that had been all right with Michael. Or so he'd told himself. He told himself that he had accepted Ripper as a sidekick who would be of use at the end of the journey and worth his now much bigger split.

But Ripper, thinking himself well-britched no doubt, cock-a-hoop with it, had begun to get too familiar. Not a tractable side-kick, and with a suddenly mocking manner to boot.

And that nickname! The nickname that Benjy had made. Michael was beginning to have more than second thoughts about Ripper, who, maybe thinking he was smarter than Michael (he was *that* dumb!) was planning a double-cross.

So be it, thought Michael. If he calls me by that name again (a name thought up by a dead man) I'll shoot the bastard.

He waited in joyful anticipation for Ripper to use *that name* again. But Ripper, maybe sensing Michael's change in demeanour, became sort of pensive, quiet even.

I'll shoot him anyway, thought Michael, chuckling inwardly. But all in good time.

★   ★   ★

Don Esteban was getting old. It was the first time he had been able to admit this to himself.

His horse seemed to be getting tired,

his steps lagging. And that didn't help. The man had ridden this trail many times before in the old, roaring days and since then. Always riding. Slower now, but always riding. This time he wished he had chosen a different means of transport.

He was greatly relieved when he saw the roofs of the small town of Daliento in the distance.

Lately things hadn't been going too well at all. There had been an irritating break in his recent plans, though that hadn't been his fault. Not entirely anyway. But maybe he'd made a mistake — again permitted himself an error in judgement in dealing once more with unpredictable Anglos who carried no honour.

His horse, smelling sustenance, quickened his pace. At the town he would be replaced and Don Etseban would be treated like a greatly honoured visitor.

Some things had not changed!

But lately the fates hadn't dealt too

kindly with Don Esteban.

He needn't have made this trip. He could have waited in his place over the border. But he had wanted to get away from there for a while and take the trail like he used to, him and a good horse.

The town wasn't as near as it seemed to be. In the dying sun it appeared like a sort of mirage: Don Esteban had seen such things in the desert areas, the badlands, which weren't so far from here.

The shimmering roofs were suddenly hidden as the trail bent to go around a grotesque outcrop of rocks which, of course, the man on the horse knew well. But suddenly they seemed to shimmer too, mirage-like, and Don Esteban, who always told himself hat he had nerves of steel, felt uncomfortable, haunted even, felt that many eyes were watching him.

13

From the rocks, Slash Conak and his boys had been watching the town and waiting for darkness. Earlier they had skirted the town widely. They were way out of their usual stamping grounds. But they had wanted a break from being chased by *rurales* and other assorted law persons, exhilarating though such occasions had sometimes been.

Slash had figured that pickings would be easier anyway in this area where they were not so well known, though he himself was certainly easy to spot.

He had gotten the scar in a street fight in Kansas when he was a kid, before, with the law on his tail even then, he'd moved further West.

The slash reached from the puckered corner of his right eye — which hadn't been affected — to the corner of his mouth. He didn't mind the nickname it had earned him. He was feared, notorious. He had killed the boy who'd given him the scar.

And now he, Slash Conak, ran the most ruthless bunch of *comancheros* who preyed on the border areas, in Mexico and, as now, further into Norte-Americano territory.

Slash wanted to take the bank in Daliento. A sweet job, he said. He had his usual regular bunch with him, hadn't chosen anybody else like he might have if they'd been raiding a rancho for instance and running cattle.

He had the renegade Apache twins who had been banished from their village for messing with other men's women and were lucky to be alive. They were poisonous bad, savage to the bone. Only their superstitious fear of their scar-faced leader kept them to a certain extent under rein, and Slash, completely amoral himself, didn't rein them too tightly, even sometimes enjoyed their depredations as did, he thought, the other two members of the regular five-man band; Sky-Eyes, half-Mexican, half-Comanche; and the other renegade Anglo, Slash's sometime partner, Lean Luke.

Slash still didn't know a hell of a lot about Luke who was as thin as a dried-out string bean, a taciturn, enigmatic individual who could only be bettered by Slash himself and who sulked if his leader upset him; wasn't just taciturn, then, but downright stone-faced until his mood changed.

They crouched in the rocks as the sun began to go down, and Sky-Eyes said, 'It will soon be time, won't it, *jefe*?' The half-breed always called Slash by the Mexican term.

Slash said, 'Don't be too impatient, *amigo*. Right now let us recheck our gear.'

They had bandannas which they could pull up over their faces and wide-brimmed sombreros which would shield and disguise their eyes. Their weapons were numerous. Five rifles, two shotguns, a couple of handguns apiece and enough bullets to start a war, a bewildering collection of knives (and one of the Apaches had a war hatchet), a lead-weighted sap which Slash carried like a toy. They all had *reatas* and quirts and, in a long boot with his Winchester, Lean Luke toted a hickory club he'd taken from a *peon* who'd tried to beat his head in with it.

Luke had broken the man's jaw with a bareknuckle blow of which any prizefighter would've been proud. But then he'd let the man live, something that Slash certainly wouldn't have done.

'There's a lone horseman coming along the trail,' Luke said.

'Do tell,' said Slash.

He had a gadget the like of which the others had never possessed. This was a small, elegant, brass telescope. He produced it, glued it to his eye, focused it.

He gave out with a little, snorting

106

exclamation, and his sidekick Luke said, 'What?'

'Godamighty,' said Slash. 'It's ol' Don Esteban Monaro. I'd know him anyplace. Fancy son-bitch on a fancy horse. Looks like he's been ridin' a long ways, though.'

'He's allus been well-britched,' said half-breed Sky-Eyes. 'Anyway, we could have some fun with the old bastard. What do you say, *jefe*?'

'All right.'

★ ★ ★

Pilgrim had spotted the town bathed eerily in a red light from the dying sun which waned even as he watched it. The rooftops were then hidden by the big rocks as the trail curved.

He was negotiating the curve when he heard the commotion from the other side of the grotesque rock outcrop.

He steered the pinto to the edge of the trail where both of them would be partially shielded, hidden. There were smaller boulders here and fallen debris which crunched under the horse's hooves. But the shouting voices from the other side of the big rocks would, Pilgrim assessed, cover any noise he was making.

Those boys sounded as if they were having a good time. But there was something mockingly menacing about the sounds also.

Pilgrim climbed down from the saddle and said, 'Stay, boy,' and, by way of reply, the pinto gave a little snort.

His master eased the handgun on his hip which was a little stiff after long hours in the saddle. He took his Winchester repeater from its scabbard and eased that into the crook of his arm, then he moved along the edge of the rocks.

He turned a craggy corner.

A man lay on the ground and others were sort of dancing around him like Indians. Indeed, two of them looked as if they were Indians. Their horses were bunched, backing on to the rocks, were kind of restless from the noise but not actually skittered.

Another horse was further on in the middle of the trail as if he had bolted to that point and then stopped. He was looking back curiously.

All this Pilgrim took in with one sweeping glance. Then one of the men — who looked like a half-breed — bent and put a rope round the neck of the man on the ground and with the end of the *reata* in his hand, made for the horses.

They were going to drag him. And they weren't making so much noise now.

Pilgrim stepped out of cover, rifle levelled, and shouted, 'Hold it there.' It was then that he realized that the man on the ground, rope round his throat, was an elderly Mexican, and he had more than a suspicion of who this might be.

The half-breed dropped his end of the rope and dived for the cover of the horses and the bigger boulders at the foot of the ugly outcrop.

In the centre somebody else moved. A gun was lifted. Pilgrim triggered the Winchester and the tall man with a scar on his face — he looked kind of familiar to Pilgrim — went flat on his back.

The pair of Indians, as alike as twin peas, ran for the horses. The rope was loose. Another man, an Anglo, raised a gun and, again, Pilgrim triggered the rifle. The man went backwards as if he'd been kicked and his gun flew in the air, the red sun catching it before it hit the ground.

The two Indians and the half-breed were on their way and Pilgrim couldn't get a shot at them. The old Mexican was in the way, pulling the *reata* from his throat, struggling to his feet. A tall, well-dressed oldster, somewhat rumpled now but smiling crookedly.

'*Gracias, señor.*'

'You're welcome.' Pilgrim moved nearer to the still figure of the man with the scarred face and bent over him. 'Slash Conak,' he said half to himself. 'I kinda thought it was.'

Slash had caught the rifle bullet in the throat and was very dead. The other Anglo was beginning to stir and Pilgrim moved over to him, went down on his haunches beside the man, kept the rifle ready.

'Joe,' the man whispered. 'Joe Pilgrim.'

A bullet in his shoulder, he was drifting in and out of consciousness; but he wasn't going to die and he still had his faculties.

Pilgrim looked closer into the lean, sunburned, almost emaciated face above the wiry body. Pilgrim fell backwards then — he winced as his butt hit the hard ground. He wasn't too well-padded on that portion of his anatomy.

His own voice was little more than a husky whisper when he said, 'Luke. Luke Profett, is that you?'

'It is, Joe. It's a long time since the old days.' The lean man began to struggle to his feet. Pilgrim grounded the rifle and began to help him. The old Mexican joined them but didn't offer to help, said, 'They were going to torture and kill me.'

'That's Esteban Monaro,' said Lean Luke.

'I figured it was,' said Joe Pilgrim. 'What I can't figure is you being here like a goddamn ghost. I thought you were back East.'

'I was. I've been in a good many places, Joe.'

'It figures. But I don't cotton to your recent friends, Luke.'

'That figures too,' said Luke. He was upright, and then he began to sway. Pilgrim caught his shoulder. 'Let's get you to town.'

The old man, returning, limping, had been collecting weapons, seemed to be festooned with them, said, 'He ought to be hanged.'

Pilgrim said, 'There are things I want to ask him. Things I've got to tell him, too.' About the death of his father Dan, back home, Pilgrim thought, about the terrible things back there.

And so many puzzles . . .

'Bear with me, old man. Help me get him on a horse.'

'You saved my life, *señor*. I will do as you say.'

14

'They're here,' said Cal Ripper.

Michael and he had adjoining rooms in the so-called hotel. Ripper had taken a short pasear and now he was back visiting Michael and had a strange look on his ugly face.

'Who's here?' Michael demanded, in his usual hectoring manner.

'Joe Pilgrim for one. And here's a strange thing: not on'y him.'

'F' Chrissakes!' Michael didn't usually indulge in profanities, but there was little doubt that his partner's halting, mysterious manner was hitting the handsome boy's nerves, no unusual thing at that.

And Ripper, ignoring him it seemed, was going on, but faster.

'He's got Don Esteban with him. And another horseman, looks like's he's wounded, that one. And if that ain't

114

Lean Luke I'll . . . ' Then Ripper was momentarily at a loss for words.

Michael said, 'Luke usually rides with Slash Conak.'

'There's another horse, looks like a body over the saddle.'

The mercurial Michael seemed to ignore this dramatic addition. 'What would Joe Pilgrim be doing with Don Esteban?' he asked himself.

'Mebbe the ol' bastard is playing both ends against the middle,' said Ripper.

Michael took note of this, asked, 'Why would he do that? We've got the *dinero* he wants.'

'Where did you arrange to meet him?' asked Ripper.

I've told this bastard too much, Michael thought. He said, 'I know where he won't be. Not in this scummy shebang. He'll go to the big boarding-house an' join his friend, Biggen.'

'They've got a body I reckon. They'll need a lawman. That fat freak Biggen ain't no lawman.'

'There ain't any real law here. Who needs it? Biggen's the mayor, ain't he? Calls himself the *alcalde*.'

'He ain't Mexican.'

'I know he ain't Mexican,' returned Michael hotly. There was little light in the room now. He scratched a lucifer and lit the lamp.

Ripper said, 'What do we do now?'

'You say looked like they had a wounded man.'

'Oh, yeh!'

'Go watch the doc's place and the undertakers'. Hell, they're almost next door to each other. But keep out of sight. I'll wait, give you a little time. I'll think o'somep'n.'

Ripper scowled but said, 'All right, if you say so.' And he left the room.

★   ★   ★

'Slash Conak,' said the lugubrious corpse-collector. 'Ain't many folk gonna miss him. When the townsfolk get to know

116

though I guess they'll come a-lookin'.'

'Bury him,' said Pilgrim shortly. 'I'll cover it.'

'I will do that,' said Don Esteban.

'You didn't shoot him.'

'I will do it.'

'Suit yourself. Let's get Luke to the doc.'

The undertaker had taken a look at the wounded man and said that Pilgrim had done a good job on him so far. Luke, conscious now, had managed a crooked grin, said he wasn't a candidate yet for the corpse-man's parlour.

The local sawbones' verdict was much the same. He put Luke to bed in his little back room which didn't have another occupant right then.

The tall old Mexican and his young companion went on to a false-fronted building which turned out to be a boarding-house. Pilgrim was introduced by Don Esteban to a small rotund individual with sleepy eyes. His manner to the don — and his young companion — could have been called fawning. His name was Biggen and the don referred to him as the *alcalde*.

Biggen made as if he was about to bow — but on account of his belly he couldn't make it. He wasn't actually of much help either, hadn't known of any strangers — or hardcases he knew — who'd moved into town lately.

Pilgrim figured the unpleasant little jasper had only just risen from an afternoon siesta. Joe wasn't interested in chit-chat, wandered over to the window and looked out onto the night with its pale stars and the lighted windows which were blossoming on all sides. No street lights, he reflected — not so's you'd notice. But he suddenly spotted something else.

A figure was lurking in the half-shadows on the sagging, splintered apology of a sidewalk opposite. Seemed to be looking at the boarding-house.

Maybe the man sensed he was, in his turn, being watched. He moved anyway, and into deeper shadows. But to Pilgrim there had seemed to be something familiar about him. It was Pilgrim's turn to move.

★ ★ ★

Ripper had been lucky enough to see Don Esteban and his companion come out of the doc's place and had tailed them discreetly to the boarding-house.

Michael had been right after all. But Ripper was still uneasy about Michael, didn't know what to do about that, never could, never had.

He watched the front of the building, thought he saw somebody at an upper window, took cover. But the figure up there — if there had been one — disappeared and there was stillness, quiet. The town wasn't jumping yet; there were few folks on the street and nobody took notice of Ripper anyway.

Cal Ripper started to do some figuring, and figuring wasn't exactly his strong point. He'd seen Don Esteban go into the house accompanied by Joe Pilgrim, and that was a mighty puzzling thing for a start.

He hadn't seen those two go into the undertaking parlour with a body, hadn't even seen them take the second man — Ripper still thought that was Lean Luke — to the doc's. But Ripper had seen Don Esteban come out of the doc's, knew they were in the hotel, obviously with the old Mexican *bandido's* fat and twisted friend, Biggen.

Michael wanted to see Don Esteban, would want to do something about Pilgrim also before Pilgrim came a-looking. Ripper decided to return to Michael. Throwing caution to the still winds he began to move out of his shadowy concealment.

A voice behind him said, 'Where'd you think you're goin', bucko?'

Ripper froze. His right hand crept down towards his belt.

Still in the same conversational, almost friendly, tone of voice, the man behind him said, 'You touch that gun, bucko, an' I'll blow your spine right through to your useless gut.'

'Pilgrim,' said Ripper huskily.

'What a clever one you are,' said Pilgrim and he moved fast then and had Ripper's gun and added, 'Now, take me to your friend Michael.'

'I don't know where he is.'

'You'd better know and you'd better move in his direction or I'll shoot you anyway and go after him myself.' The voice wasn't friendly now, not even conversational.

Ripper moved and Pilgrim went on talking softly. Mockingly now. 'I know somep'n you don't, bucko.'

Ripper took the bait. 'Whassat?'

'Michael killed your sidekick Dack. Benjy told me before he died.'

'Benjy's dead too?' croaked Ripper.

'You better believe it, bucko.'

They went up the back stairs, the way Ripper had come out of the hotel. Michael's door was shut. Ripper's mind was in turmoil. He felt he didn't care what happened to Michael now, the treacherous coyote. He wanted to save his own skin any way he could, and that was the only fact he was sure about. He knocked on Michael's door as Pilgrim had ordered him to do.

There was no sound from inside and Pilgrim poked a gun barrel in Ripper's back and Ripper knocked again. But still there was no answer.

'Open it,' Pilgrim hissed.

'But . . . '

'Open it. Or I'll shoot you an' blast my way in.'

Ripper did as he was told.

Nothing happened. The room was empty.

'He's gone,' said Ripper plaintively, 'and he's took the saddle-bags with him.'

'The bank money?'

'Yeh.'

'He had all of it?'

'Yeh.'

'Jumpin' cats,' said Pilgrim. 'You're a goddamn idiot, bucko.'

Ripper didn't argue with him.

15

Ripper said that Michael would go for the border and Don Esteban backed him on this.

The elderly Mexican confessed to the young man who had saved his life that Michael had promised to bring money to buy a big part of the rancho's herd before the stock became even more depleted. The Mexican *jefe*, himself once a *bandido*, had suffered sorely in recent times from the attacks of border rustlers, *comancheros* and renegade Indians.

The oldster, although he still behaved the way an honourable man should do, with independence and pride, was a sick man and wanted to get a *hacienda* further back in his beloved Mexico, away from the warlike borderlands where human wolves roamed and pillaged, and spend his last days with his two daughters and their families.

'I should not have dealt with such a man as Michael,' he said, 'and rode to meet him almost secretly as I did. I was hiding things from myself.'

He knew the full story now. 'I will ride with you to find this man who would murder his own people,' he added.

These words were almost echoed by Luke Profett, 'Lean' Luke to the border desperadoes who knew him well. The doc said Luke wasn't fit to ride. Pilgrim didn't think it was fitting either. Ripper had already been incarcerated in a small blockhouse, guarded by two of Alcalde Biggen's 'volunteers' which would serve as a jail until Ripper was handed over to territory law.

Luke, who seemed to be miraculously forcing himself to mend, gave his word to Pilgrim, an old boyhood friend, that he would not try to escape, that he only wanted to get the man who had killed his father, Dan.

There was no time to waste.

Ultimately, three men rode.

A sick old Mexican, a wounded ne'er-do-well, and a professional gun-fighter with an implacable resolve.

Lean Luke had something to add to what he had already said. But he wasn't overplaying his hand, was just being careful.

'We've still got to watch out for those three,' he said. 'Sky-Eyes and the Apache twins. They'll want your scalp. And mine too, if they see me with you. You killed their *jefe*. And you shamed them as well.'

'Sky-Eyes?' Pilgrim said. 'Ain't that Injun too?'

'He's half-Comanche. Maybe Sky-Eyes is sort of a tribal name, I dunno.'

'I thought Apaches and Comanches were natural enemies, that the Comanches steal Apache women to sell them to the *bordello* owners over the border.'

'I heard that too. But the twins ain't real braves. They ain't even normal Injuns. They're maniacal renegades. It'll be a feudal thing with those three. Getting you, banding together against a *gringo* who did 'em wrong, an Anglo who shamed 'em.'

The morning mist was slowly drifting away and the burgeoning sun peered down from above. It was going to be a good day but a damn' hot one. They made good time while they could and they read sign from time to time (all three of them had the expertise) but maybe not with great success. Until the Fates smiled briefly upon them.

If only indirectly, Don Esteban lent a hand too. Whether for good or bad he was an honoured personage in this territory.

They, the three of them, ran across a couple of *peons* driving a small, bleating bunch of mangy sheep. The two keepers recognized the don, however, and took off their wide-brimmed hats and bowed before him and he asked them a question in their own language and got an answer. Lean Luke translated the answer even before Don

Esteban could do so.

These two boys had passed on the narrow trail up ahead, on a lone horse a man they described as *bonito greengo*, which made Joe Pilgrim, who knew some Spanish, laugh somewhat immoderately to the amazement of his two companions.

Don Esteban stroked the two boys' hands with *dinero*. The ill-assorted company separated, going in different directions in two segments, and the sour smell of sheep drifted off from the nostrils of the trio making for the border, the old Mexican leading the way now.

Pilgrim caught up with him. Don Esteban's dark, hawk-like face looked drawn. Pilgrim asked, 'How did you first get to know Michael Tagwell?'

'One day he and two other riders came across the big river. One of the men was the *gringo* called Ripper, the other I think called Dack . . . '

'You have a good memory.'

'Their horses were blown and I sold

127

them fresh ones, very good ones. Michael visited me afterwards at times, sometimes alone, sometimes with the other two.'

Lean Luke caught up. He still wore his left arm in a sling, had been told by the doc in Daliento, reluctant to let him ride, to keep the sling in position at all times. Luckily, the wounded shoulder was the left one, and Luke was a right-handed man.

The Luke that Pilgrim had known in the old days had never been a shooter, but this one obviously was, his side arm, though not new, well worn, low slung and in perfect condition. Right now, though, its owner didn't look any healthier than the old Mexican did.

* * *

Pete Teller and his daughter Arabella had a mid-morning visitor, a smart young man in store clothes in a gig drawn by two high-stepping ponies.

He was obviously an Easterner,

beautifully spoken, but arrogant, looking down from his perch at the elderly man and the girl who had come out to meet him.

On his closer look at the girl his eyes became admiring, but then took on a calculating glint. Obviously he wasn't used to seeing a beautiful filly in men's pants: possibly he thought that such a lovely hoyden would be fine game for him.

Such a handsome buck.

Arabella didn't say anything, but her courteous father invited the visitor to step down, bide a while.

The stranger stepped down on fancy riding boots which were almost knee-length. But he said he couldn't stay, that he was calling on every rancher in the territory, had already visited some of the Tellers' neighbours.

It was at this point that Arabella drew her father's attention to the four horsemen who had appeared on the rise above, on the top of the slope down which the young Easterner had driven his gig a few minutes before.

'I don't seem to recognize them,' said Pete.

'Me neither,' said his daughter.

'They're friends of mine,' the young man said. 'You might call them my entourage.'

'Want 'em to come visiting?' asked Pete and, whether the visitor noticed or not she didn't know, Arabella detected the mocking note that had crept into the older man's voice.

'They're all right,' the young man said, and he introduced himself as Carstairs, a name that seemed to suit him, Arabella thought. She wondered whether, at the other places, Carstairs had had his entourage right here with him and what the neighbours' attitudes had been. In the main, they were peaceable folk, but many of them weren't as courteous, easygoing and hospitable as her father tended to be.

The four horsemen stayed where they were, like so many equestrian statues, as the young Easterner made his speil.

His father was the managing director of the firm that wished to turn this territory into a great ranching community for the benefit of all.

Horse-shit, thought Arabella, but she didn't speak, wasn't too given to profanity anyway.

The monetary offer which Carsairs spoke of now was the biggest the Tellers had heard and was generous, had they wanted to sell the ranch that is.

Pete, of course, turned the offer down, gently but firmly, hiding the steel which his daughter knew was in him. Carstairs handed the older man a business card and said, 'You can get in touch with me if you change your mind.' Then he climbed into his gig and turned his ponies around and, even as he did so, the four horsemen disappeared from the top of the rise.

'Damn' fancy-pants,' said Arabella, giving way at last.

'Daughter!' said Pete in mock anger.

But back in the house he added, 'That young gink didn't appeal to you at all, did he, honey?'

'Not a bit.'

'I know the type you prefer,' said Pete, and they both knew the particular type to which he referred, even maybe the particular man.

'Sometimes things don't work out,' added Pete softly.

'But sometimes they do.'

'Granted.' Then Pete changed the subject. 'I wonder if we'll see purty Mr Carstairs again, or any of his boys.'

The wondering hung in the air, had no answering.

* * *

It was night again and Cal Ripper was still in the blockhouse.

He had seen two separate guards, as both of them had brought him food. There was always at least one of them on guard outside, as far as he could see anyway: there were no windows in the back of the blockhouse, only in front.

Once he had seen fat Biggen; who called himself an *alcalde* for Pete's sake! The other boys seemed to do what Biggen said. Once Ripper had seen three boys, one of them a bit fancier and bossier-looking than the other two. Maybe he was more of a Biggen confidant.

The other two, though burly and mean-looking, Ripper had pegged as barflies. Maybe at night they took turns to go get a drink.

One of them always paced with a sawn-off shotgun, a weapon that anybody with any sense didn't mess with at all. The other man had a belt-gun but didn't seem to carry anything else.

The blockhouse had evidently been used as a storeroom and though it seemed now to be full of nothing but valueless junk, it smelled of onions. And Ripper didn't like onions. He watched for a longish absence of the big man with the sawn-off, watched the big man's Colt-slung partner who wasn't so big or quite so mean-looking.

The blockhouse door was stout, ideal for the purpose for which it was now being used. There were two windows, one at each side of the door, but they were narrow and, Ripper figured, hardly wide enough to allow his body through even if he smashed every bit of glass and sash. He'd be shot dead before that: the thought of a shotgun blast blowing his body to bloody shreds made him shake like he had a killing ague.

He was not a bright man but, in common with his wolfish kind, had a well-honed talent for self-preservation coupled with an animal cunning. He was not a noisy man. He watched and waited. In the dead of that night his chance came.

Outside, the two guards were suddenly arguing. Then the bigger one strode away, his sawn-off sloped over his shoulder.

Ripper lost sight of the other one, figured he was leaning against the wall, or maybe even sitting against it someplace.

Ripper went to the window and craned his neck and couldn't see anything, crossed to the other one. He saw a faint glow through the glass. He craned his neck again and he almost gasped.

The guard was sitting on his butt with his back comfortably against the log wall at the side and below the window. He was smoking, though his head was almost sunk on his breast and he was maybe dozing also, his cigarette dangling from his lips.

Ripper figured he ought to move the son-bitch somehow before he set himself on fire.

Ripper looked about in the darkness for a weapon, being as quiet as he could, bending, feeling.

His fingers closed over a length of timber and he carried it lovingly over to the window. He had, of course, been divested of all his weapons. But he still had his riding gloves tucked in back of his belt where he'd once had a small back-up over-and-under pistol also.

He donned the gloves. He craned his neck. The guard's cigarette had dropped from his lips and lay at his side, glowing minutely. So the bastard hadn't got himself burned. But he sure as hell was now in the land of Nod.

Ripper smashed the window with his improvised club then swung it out and downwards onto the sleeping man's head, knocking his slouch hat even further over his eyes. The man fell over on his side, his hat beside him then. He lay still.

Ripper knew he had to work mighty fast. If he made too much noise and it was heard he could be a gone goose. He smashed the glass completely, feeling a sliver cut into his wrist but ignoring it.

He got his body out finally by twisting it sideways. But then he was stuck. He could, however, reach the unconscious body — and the man's belt-gun was holstered on that side.

Ripper stretched, groaned. His gloved

hands closed over the butt of the gun and he drew it out, drew himself out and away from the window, moved a little way to the door, levelled the gun, thumbed the hammer, blew the lock off.

With the blast, the door swung open and Ripper eeled through it. Crouching, he went round to the back of the building, then paused to get his bearings.

The shot would have been heard. He would be expected to run out of town — if he had a horse. And, as far as he knew, his own mount was still at the livery stables.

He swung away round the backs of town, away from the trail. He was getting his bearings. He ran up the narrow alley which ran alongside the main saloon in town and peered around the corner at the other end.

As he expected, folks were running down the street away from him and towards the blockhouse. They were on foot. There were horses at the hitching rack outside the saloon, one of them pretty close to Ripper. And momentarily the frontage of the saloon was devoid of people.

Ripper came out of concealment, mounted the startled beast, set him at a gallop, which wasn't hard to accomplish. Out the back-ass end of town. And then a detour . . .

He heard no shouts, no shooting.

He figured he might know where Michael was making for.

Part Three

Retribution

16

Michael's mind had been a bit mixed up since he left Daliento. He only knew that he had had to get out of there. Get away from Ripper too.

But then there was all the money of course. Hot dog!

He was cock-a-hoop now, hitting the lonesome trail with bags full of rich boodle.

He didn't figure Don Esteban, couldn't understand what that old fox could be doing with Joe Pilgrim. But sharp-shooter Pilgrim, who had the tenacity of a hound dog, was a person whom Michael didn't want to meet up with, and he even admitted that to himself now.

He knew where he was going, him and the big boodle. Hell, Don Esteban wasn't the only fish in the sea, the big river actually, either side of it. And

Michael knew of a place . . .

The night had been dark and cloudy, but now the moon was up and bathed horse and rider in a yellow light. He had looked back from time to time and hadn't seen anybody on his tail. In fact, the only folk he had passed, and that had been much earlier, had been Mexican *peons* with a bunch of sheep.

The sheep had stunk. And their keepers, while greeting Michael nervously in their own tongue, had gazed at him as if they thought all *gringos* were devils from Hell. And maybe they were. Michael smiled to himself. Speak for yourself, brother, he thought.

Ahead of him was a bend in the trail, rocks scattered around it, boulders not particularly large. Michael looked back along the moonlit trail. *Nothing*.

When he faced forward again there were three horsemen at the bend of the trail. They looked like Indians.

They were still, something incredibly menacing about them.

Michael took one of his hands off his

reins. But if he was about to do something it was useless. He saw the steel flashing in the moonlight, then it became embedded in his shoulder, the force of the blow knocking him backwards so that he lost his balance. He hit the ground and became partially stunned, but then he looked up and the moonlight was in his eyes and the horsemen were limned against it, surrounding him.

★ ★ ★

It was the twins' idea. They were still sold on getting the tall, sharp-shooting Anglo who had bested them and killed the man they looked up to, though himself an Anglo, but like a god-figure to their superstitious souls, Slash Conak.

Sky-Eyes didn't like the idea. The big haul of *dinero* would compensate for any lack of vengeance against the gunfighter. But the stupid twins didn't seem to bother about the money and

Sky-Eyes knew he had to go along with them, figured they were capable of cutting his throat and scattering the money to the four winds if they felt like it. They liked the wild trails, the killing and the torture far more than any money.

So they didn't torture the money-man. Not yet. They took him with them and left a trail, and Sky-Eyes tagged along. He was half-Indian himself and had his cunning side. Maybe the Apache twins' idea was a good one after all — maybe Sky-Eyes could get all of the money for himself and shake the law — *or whatever* — off his back and hightail over the border and live in peace and plenty, be a don even like that old *hijo de puta*, Esteban Monaro.

★   ★   ★

After skirting the town widely and as quietly as possible, Ripper rode harder than ever, only pausing a couple of times and hearing no sounds of pursuit.

The horse he had stolen was a fast-moving not too heavy dun stallion who didn't seem to mind having a new rider. He was a good acquisition, but all Ripper had besides was a Colt .45 with only five shots in it, no other ammunition. There was a saddle scabbard on the horse, but no rifle; nobody but an idiot would leave a long gun in its sheath on a horse outside a saloon.

Ripper wondered who the horse's owner had been and whether this was some proud cowboy's best mount. But he soon forgot, had more important things to think about.

He remembered when Michael and he and Dack had pulled a job in a bank on the other side of the Rio Grande and it had been somewhat of a fizzle, not much *dinero* in the haul and a quick reaction from townies and the *rurales* on the tails of the three robbers.

They had hidden out in a valley and the *rurales* had gone right by and Michael had said that some day he was going to build a ranch in that valley.

Was that what the new money had been for? Was that why Michael had robbed his father's own bank? In Mexico, money could buy anything — and nobody would recognize or question a rich *gringo* who last time he was in that territory had worn a black scarf over his face.

Fleetingly, Ripper had reflected that there might be other seekers between him and Michael. But he told himself that, being one man alone, he'd be able to evade them.

* * *

Pete Teller said, 'We haven't set eyes on Pink or Seal since way before that young Eastern fancy-pants called Carstairs came a visiting, him an' his four boys up on the rise.'

'I guess they're staying in town,' said Arabella Teller.

'They haven't been doing that lately. If they'd intended, I reckon they would've told us first.'

146

Arabella made a little sound with her lips, but she couldn't argue with what her father had just said.

'Well, it's time we got our heads down anyway, gal. If they come in the night we'll hear 'em.'

They didn't come in the night, but they turned up the following morning just after the Tellers rose. That would be about the usual time Pink and Seal appeared if they'd been staying in town. But this time they hadn't been staying in town. And they had a tale to tell.

The day before, they had been bringing in a couple of wandering dogies and their momma when they spotted the man in the fancy gig with his mounted entourage. Luckily, the two boys and the beef had been out of sight.

They had left the beef behind, hoping the big one and the two little ones wouldn't stray again. They had tailed the strangers and hidden in a clump of trees looking out at the top of the rise where the four horsemen had halted and the man in the gig had gone down the hill.

'We saw the fancy-pants come back,' said Seal. 'An' we tailed the whole bunch of 'em, tailed 'em a long way.'

'Yeh, boss,' said Pink. 'Do you remember that ghost town about a dozen miles from here, mebbe more?'

'I know.'

'There's a small army bivouacked there. Gunfighters I guess; looked that way. Even looks like some o' the place has been rebuilt, made more sheltered and comfortable anyway.'

'That fancy son-bitch is planning somep'n all right — beggin' your pardon, Miss Arabella.'

The girl smiled, said, 'Granted,' mockingly.

'We got outa there, got back as soon as we could, didn't think we'd been spotted, nobody follered us anyway.'

'Yeh,' said the other boy, 'an' on our way back we bumped into ol' Swede who runs the smallholding by the creek. He'd done the rounds and he said nobody did a deal with that bunch.'

'Did you tell Swede about the folks at the ghost town?'

'Nope. Figured we ought to tell you first.'

'Good. But now everybody will have to be told, pronto. If that mob are really comin' outa the woods at last we'll have to sort of beat 'em to it, some way.'

'We figured . . . '

'We guessed . . . ' The two boys were almost in unison, and raring to go. They knew their boss was an old Indian fighter, a grand man, but not one to be pushed in any way at all.

17

They found the bloodstained knife on the trail and the faded red, looped scarf which appeared to have been used as a headband.

Lean Luke said, 'That knife belonged to one of the Apache twins. Hell, I could never tell them apart. That one had a collection of knives. I recognize this blade 'cos of the scraggy handle. He used it for throwing practice. Maybe he dumped it. Maybe he just dropped it. I guess the headband belonged to one o' them bucks as well.'

Pilgrim looked about him, said, 'Maybe they came to grief somehow.' He got down from his horse.

'I doubt it,' said Luke. 'Not those two. Unless maybe they had a run-in with Sky-Eyes. He ain't all Injun — he'd want the *dinero*.'

Luke was down from his saddle now

also, but Don Esteban hadn't moved. He sat with head bowed and didn't speak.

'We can track.' Pilgrim climbed back into the saddle and Luke followed suit.

All three were pretty good trackers, and now the old man began to take more interest, said, 'This used to be good cattle country till sheep were run on it.'

Luke said, 'We ain't seen any more woollies since that last lot on the trail.'

'It isn't good enough for sheep now, not even them. But I can still smell them.'

Of course you can, you old goat, Pilgrim reflected, that's what you did when you were a boy, I guess, a low *peon* on the other side of the big river. Were all the years in between now turning to ashes?

'Injuns don't usually make tracks,' said Luke softly. 'And those damn' twins are like ghosts.'

'Yeh,' said Pilgrim. 'Let's spread out a mite but keep in sight of each other.'

151

It was he who first spotted the tumbledown cabin which maybe in cattle-running days had served as a line hut. He motioned his two companions to halt.

Nothing moved, and now even the three men seemed to be holding their breath. Then Luke, who was nearest to Pilgrim, gave a little hiss between clenched teeth, beating Pilgrim, who had also spotted what Luke had seen: a lone figure seated on the ground with its back against the sagging cabin wall.

All three men hit the ground which was lumpy and rock-strewn. The old don, with his well-honed instinct for preservation (he didn't mean to die quite yet) was suddenly almost as agile as his two young partners.

Noise exploded from the disused cabin and bullets zipped over the heads of the three men, the report awakening the echoes. In a short lull Pilgrim shouted, 'I want Michael alive.'

He had recognized the man seated against the wall and figured that the other two had also. A still figure stripped to the waist, legs stretched out, feet together, hands hidden. But no mark on him, so maybe he was still alive, hands rawhided behind his back, ankles tethered also.

A careless trail, purposely so. Then bait. Ambush. But they'd half-expected something like this and they weren't badly covered. The cabin stood in what had once been a wooded clearing but there'd been a fire there at some time or other and the trees were blackened and stunted, though some of them were showing fresh foliage. The cabin backed on to trees which hadn't been touched by the fire and looked as if it hadn't suffered heat either, just the ravages of neglect and the elements.

The three men on the outside had adequate cover, which they made good use of when the shooting started again, retaliating, peppering the shack, trying not to hit the figure against the wall, unmoving, unspeaking.

Pilgrim figured that the man called

Sky-Eyes was well set inside the cabin. But Pilgrim wasn't so sure about the two Apaches: they were of a guerrilla-type fighting race, used to battling outdoors, moving like the in-fighting athletes and acrobats they were.

Still and all, maybe this ambush had been the twins' idea after all, crazy renegades that they were, not wholly belonging to either Indian, Mexican, or Anglo. It was hard to tell how many men were in the cabin anyway. Pilgrim and his two partners had to get nearer. He signalled. They had anticipated him. Using all the cover they could find, they moved off and outwards a little, and Pilgrim tried to keep in the middle as much as he could without risking getting his head shot off.

The sun was hot and it was behind the three crawling men. Their horses were behind them, in cover. The harsh sunlight blazed on the shack and they saw every sagging line of it and the eyes of the man against the wall, open, staring.

And the man moved, twisted, lurched, fell forward on his face, then lay still again. A lesser target anyway.

*   *   *

The old line shack wasn't such good cover as it might have been. The walls were thin and, in places, bullets could easily penetrate them. There was an old bunk, mildewed and stinking which Sky-Eyes and the two Apaches had turned up and dragged against the glassless, lopsided window. To use this sorry piece of furniture adequately the three men had to crouch side by side.

There was a pot-bellied stove, its stovepipe angling perilously upwards and through the partially shattered roof. The whole structure, stove and all, appeared as if it would fall in upon itself at any moment as the gunfire reverberated in and around it, and the slugs came through the timberwork like spiteful hornets.

Sky-Eyes had tried crouching behind

the stove, but from that position he couldn't see anything to shoot at. The twins, and in the main this caper had been their idea, seemed to be enjoying themselves. More than anything in the world they loved fighting and killing and seemed to have no conception of their own personal danger.

Renegades or not, right now they were all Indian, all Apache: fighting was their glory, and dying fighting their enemies would be a glory also.

Crazy Apaches, Sky-Eyes thought, forgetting momentarily that half of him belonged to a warlike race, the Comanches, as savage as any Apache. But hell, he should be fighting these two, not parding with 'em!

He was at the end of the tumbled bunk. A zinging slug almost took his ear off. He was half-crouching and he flinched, lost his balance, fell over backwards.

The back of his head hit the twin saddle-bags that had been thrown carelessly on the floor. All that money treated like shit: the thought exploded in Sky-Eyes' brain. His gun was still in his right hand. He grabbed the saddle-bags with his other hand and he clambered to his feet.

He had already ascertained that there was a back way out of the ruined line shack. Not a back door, a hole in the wall, ragged, with brush poking through it from outside. But big enough to let a crawling man through. A bolthole.

Carrying the bags, he lurched towards the hole. And one of the twins said something in his own guttural tongue. Sky-Eyes whirled, his gun lifting.

One of the twins was on his feet. Sky-Eyes fired the gun, felt it buck satisfying in his fist, knew it was true. But, then, even as the buck began to fall, hit full in the middle of the chest, Sky-Eyes saw the flash of the knife.

The other twin, turned now, had thrown the weapon from a crouching position. Sky-Eyes could hardly tell these two apart. But the second one was the wizard with knives. I should've shot him first, thought Sky-Eyes as the steel bit into his heart. Then he was falling. Then he was dead.

The remaining twin retrieved his knife from the body, wiped it, stashed it in the back of his belt where he had two more. He looked at the two bodies, his face expressionless. He picked up the stuffed saddlebags which he knew held *dinero*, though he hadn't attached any importance to this fact before.

But he knew this haul could buy him plenty women over the border. And much more than that . . .

18

There had been a single shot. Then all shooting had stopped. Pilgrim had shouted at Luke, 'That one shot came from inside the cabin. Cover me.'

Luke gestured that he understood, glanced at Don Esteban who nodded. Pilgrim eeled from cover to cover and nothing happened, but then he reached the open space in front of the hut and there was no cover at all.

Crouching low, he did a running zig-zag. Nobody shot at him. In front of the shattered building the still body of Michael Tagwell lay on its face.

Pilgrim went past the still form and through the door, round the edge of the jamb and was almost on his belly now, his gun pointing out in front of him like an accusing finger. When nothing happened, he straightened up, feeling kind of foolish.

All that was left in the sorry interior of this sorry place were two bodies, one whiteish, one Indian. There were no saddle-bags.

There was a sort of bolthole right opposite Pilgrim, broken branches poking through. Stooping, Pilgrim went through. There was a narrow, partially covered trail in the trees and some evidence of a hurrying body passing that way.

He heard the hoofbeats: they were muffled, even distant. More than one horse. The second Indian was to hell and gone, and the spare horseflesh with him. And them money bags. This was no damn' stupid Injun, not at all! Pilgrim went back the way he'd come.

The old Mexican and the Anglo with his arm in a sling were bending over Michael Tagwell. The old man turned him over and, as Pilgrim joined them, made a small exclamation in his own language, pointing downwards. On Michael's shoulder was a strange, whitish pad of dried and sun-faded moss, adhering there by earth, dried mud maybe. From a distance it would have been difficult to see this on the body, and the man had looked as if he was completely bare to the waist and unmarked.

Michael was still alive and, as the old man began to undo the bonds at wrists and ankles, he opened his eyes.

Three pairs of eyes looked down at him, one pair in a lean face, not so easily recognizable as the other two but still strangely familiar — one pair of eyes full of hate.

Don Esteban, whom Michael knew quite well, spoke in English now, pedantically and almost as if he were talking to himself. 'Who can fathom the Indian mind? I've known a lot of Apaches, good and bad. An Apache treated that wound, which might have happened when Michael ran into them. Then he was put out here.'

'Bait,' said Pilgrim sardonically. 'They wanted to keep him in trim till we got here, hoped that then they could take good care of the rest of us as well.'

'They should've killed him right off,' Lean Luke said. 'Save me the trouble. This bastard killed my father.'

'Luke Profett,' said Michael, astonished; and Luke pointed the muzzle of a .45 down at him.

'Don't do it, Luke,' said Pilgrim.

'You ain't totin' a badge, Joe,' said Luke, still pointing the gun at the staring man on the ground.

'No. But I've got to take him back. Other folk are involved. Him and his boys also killed old friend, Tim Molan, whose widow Ruthie is grieving back there.'

The gun in Luke's hand wavered. 'Ruthie married Tim?'

'Yeh. The boys wounded a deputy as well. But no law could chase 'em this far, outa jurisdiction, and who'd get 'em here, eh? I've got to take the money back too, and it ain't here. Sky-Eyes and one o' the Indians are both dead. The other one hightailed it with the money . . . '

'We heard horses,' put in Don Esteban.

'Yeh, all their horses I guess. But only one man.'

'What do we do with him then?' asked Luke, sardonically. 'Let him free like a bird?'

Before Pilgrim could answer this, Don Esteban put in again, 'I'll stay with him. I have to rest, my *amigos*. Tie him again and I will stay in the hut with him. Just leave me a few provisions and water. I will not let him escape. I will stay here till you come back.'

Pilgrim looked at Luke who had his gun by his side now. The lean man said brusquely, 'Tie him then, drag him in there.' He jerked a thumb in the direction of the disused cabin. 'Then let us get going.'

Michael began to protest, but Luke raised the gun as if to pistol-whip him and he shut up. 'Roll over,' Luke snarled. Michael did as he was told. Pilgrim had the rawhide, bent to his task.

★ ★ ★

'Do you think we can trust that ol' goat?' said Luke as Pilgrim and he hit the trail again.

'Have to, I guess. I wouldn't want him tagging along any more with us. I don't think he could stand the pace. How about you? How's that shoulder?'

'I'll be all right.'

'So what brought you to this neck of the woods?' Pilgrim asked mildly. But his eyes were still on the trail as he looked for sign and the question had come out almost as a sort of afterthought.

'It's kind of a long story,' said Luke, 'and not a particularly edifying one, as you imagine, now you know the kind of characters I've been ridin' with in recent times.'

'You still talk like an educated man when you remember to do that.'

'Yes. I went East to train to be a teacher. An English teacher no less. I got married to a fellow student who was taking chemistry. I didn't know she was a bitch straight from Hell. She cuckolded — Hell knows . . . Anyway, finally she ran off with another man but, so I couldn't follow right off, she poisoned me. It's a wonder she didn't kill me. She should've done . . . '

'This way,' said Pilgrim, interrupting. 'Keep your head down.'

'Well, I heard that her new man was a businessman who was moving West heading a cattle-buying combine. I came looking, didn't find hide nor hair, ran out of money, got in bad company.' Luke gave a little spurt of harsh laughter. 'That's what they call it, isn't it? Helped rob a bank. Got nothing! My two partners got killed, an' later I got mixed up with Conak, Sky-Eyes an' the twins . . . ' He paused.

'There are some bluffs ahead, Joe. Prime bush-whack cover.'

'I see.'

'I'd only joined Slash a little time ago, Joe. They were harassing folk like Don Esteban, who was a *comanchero*

165

himself to begin with.'

'So I've heard. Anyway, mebbe Slash felt he needed a *gringo* sidekick.'

'I decided I disliked the man pretty much. I was figuring . . . '

'Split! Down!' yelled Pilgrim, who had spotted a glint of steel in the rocks.

As the two riders quickly separated, crouching low in their saddles, a bullet zinged between them, nearer to Luke, could have been in his head had he stayed in line.

19

The Apache twin let out a small string of curses in a mixture of his own tongue and bastardized Spanish, the latter being the most profane and colourful. He bowed his head, shamed because he had missed his target. He had not at first understood why Lean Luke, as the scar-faced gringo *jefe* had called him, had made a turnabout. But he figured he did now, his eyes alighting on the money at his feet. Luke and the other *gringo*, the quick-shooting *caballero*, were after the money. White men loved money so much!

They had given him no time. No time to even grieve, if only briefly, over his dead brother. He felt like remaining now with his shamed head bowed and throwing dirt over that head and over himself and shouting a dirge at the mocking sun that blazed down at him.

He wished it was the night — he did not mind fighting by night.

The two horsemen were coming fast, using their handguns past their horses' necks. Bullets hit the rock, some of them coming perilously close, ricocheting. The Apache raised his rifle again, a stolen Winchester with which he was pretty good. But he knew the aiming would not be so good now.

He gave a shrill cry, throwing his head back and his voice to the sky, although the sun almost blinded him. He lowered his head again. The man called Sky-Eyes had killed the brother. A man who was more Anglo than Indian. And now there was another one down there, Luke, with the *caballero* who was another hated Anglo.

They were coming closer and they should be killed.

He half-rose to his feet and levelled the rifle, aimed it at Lean Luke whom he hated the most, the man who had once been a *compadre* — Sky-Eyes had called him that — but was now nothing more than a despised white enemy.

Before he could squeeze the trigger he was hit in a spot in the middle of his body where his scuffed leather vest was parted to reveal his flesh, a vulnerable place between his breastbone and his belly.

He was thrown backwards and fell on his back, but rolled away from the glare of the sun which now seemed to be mocking him.

It was a bad wound he knew, feeling the pain welling up, bubbling inside — but now he made no sound.

His horse was behind him, sheltered by a tall boulder shaped like the crown of a tall sombrero.

He crawled around the rock, after drawing his vest across the wound and using the thongs to fasten it very tightly. He climbed into the saddle and the good horse carried him away from the place.

He left the *dinero* behind. *What was dinero?*

Perhaps he could get back to his

people. Perhaps they would take him — to live, or soon to die.

★ ★ ★

There was blood on the saddle-bags when Pilgrim picked them up, intact and full of riches. 'He's hit and he has hightailed,' Pilgrim said. 'We haven't the time to chase him.' He slung the bags over the front of his saddle.

They did not drive their horses too hard on their way back to the ruined line hut. They had done enough hard riding.

Looking at Luke, Pilgrim saw that there were rivulets of sweat running down the almost emaciated face. 'You all right?' he asked. 'That shoulder botherin' you?'

'Not too much, Joe, thanks,' said the lean man. 'But I've been sick. Time back, I mean. Back East — after the trouble with the woman.' He grinned mirthlessly, looking at his old neighbour. 'Extra trouble. Lung trouble.

Another reason for coming West I guess — and it worked. But I still get kinda tired now and then, and this wound can't have helped. I talked to the doc at Daliento about it, didn't tell anybody else. That was another reason he didn't want me to take this trail. But he said the lungs were pretty fine . . . '

Luke paused, as if cogitating with himself. Then he went on, 'As for the woman — I've shut her out of my mind like she was part of another life.'

Pilgrim reflected that in the old days Luke and him had never been what you might call bosom friends, but they had gotten along all right. Pilgrim hadn't been surprised when Luke took off. He had done more than a mite of taking off himself.

Luke had been a loner, and didn't that make him and Luke two of a kind? Now he felt drawn to the man. Himself, he sure as hell was no angel. He said impulsively, 'You're goin' home.'

'Am I?'

'Yes.'
'All right.'

* * *

The old Mexican was dozing again. Sitting on the floor with the rifle across his knees and his back against the sagging wall.

Michael began to work on his bonds again.

The old man looked washed out. Had he known Michael was working to get out, he would've kept alert, and the old bastard would have been dangerous.

Michael had already tried the most obvious verbal ploy, calling on Don Esteban's earlier friendship, asking for a chance, just one small chance. But the old don had been stony-eyed and adamant. As if Joe Pilgrim was his long-lost son or something — and that was ludicrous. Joe Pilgrim had saved his life, so he said, going honorable as all get-out, the goddamn old twister.

But, even if his resolve was the same, his ageing body had let him down. He had started in his sleep, made noises. But now he was well gone and his breath, though heavy, was even.

With fingers that were torn and aching, Michael worked on the rawhide at his wrists and finally the strands parted. He brought his hands round carefully in front of him, slowly, his shoulders and arms aching too, with the efforts he had made, some of the fingers on his right hand torn and bleeding. His wounded shoulder gnawed as if bitten.

But he was triumphant. And the bonds at his ankles were a comparatively easy task. It was when they were parting, however, as if some sixth sense had warned him, Don Esteban woke up.

He lifted the rifle.

Michael rolled sideways, the pain exploding in his wounded shoulder like a blast of fire. But the bullet went past him, the report of the long gun sounding like a cannon-shot in the enclosed place.

Pain and desperation drove Michael. Before the old don could trigger the rifle again the younger man was upon him.

Hands gripped the old man's throat. His head was banged again and again against the wall, shaking it, making the dust fall. His eyes closed, and his assailant let him go and he slumped in a heap and the dust settled.

Michael rose slowly to his feet. His head was swimming and blood trickled across his chest from his shoulder. The 'big medicine' mixture that the Indian twin had pressed there was still partially intact but the wound was open again.

Michael took Don Esteban's rifle and his handgun and he staggered outside and mounted the old man's horse, a fine stallion who'd had a good rest and was more than ready to start moving again.

★ ★ ★

'That was a shot all right,' said Lean Luke. He urged the horse to a greater pace and Pilgrim followed suit.

They hit the back of the old hut in a scramble and a cloud of dust and their guns were in their hands. They tumbled from the saddle, Pilgrim in front now, Luke behind him, moving a little unsteadily.

Pilgrim, crouching, went through the jagged gap in the back wall.

When Luke got inside the structure, Pilgrim was bending over the old man slumped against the wall. Pilgrim turned, straightening. 'He's still alive, don't look like he's been shot. Wait here an' look after him.'

'All right, Joe.'

Pilgrim had to go through the back again to get his horse. He steered the willing beast around to the front of the cabin and across the scrubby clearing.

The shot that Luke and he had heard had sounded like a rifle, obviously the one Don Esteban had held and which Michael had taken, the don's belt-gun too, Pilgrim had noticed.

He pushed the pinto, but the beast was mighty good over the uneven ground.

Michael couldn't be far ahead, Pilgrim figured, still stripped to the waist under the sun, though that was waning now.

A desperate, half-naked wounded man. A crazy man . . .

20

Despite the reality of his escape from a situation which might have culminated in his having his neck stretched, Cal Ripper's triumph had a sort of aftermath, a sort of let down. He didn't know whether he'd ever catch up with Michael. Also, although he didn't like to admit it, he knew that Michael was a better pistoleer than he and might best him after all. Also, as Michael knew more folks in the border territories than Ripper did, might even be able to call himself an important man (he certainly thought he was), he might have already picked up other *compadres* who, for a stroke of *dinero*, would be more than willing to do his dirty work for him.

There was a lot at stake, a golden pick-up for the man left alive.

A tired Ripper. And a tired horse too. A stolen one but a good one. Only horseflesh, though, and a good heart — granted — but not tireless. A horse that began to flag, even to veer and stumble a bit, and hit a patch of uneven land with sharp rocks and hidden pitfalls and then began to limp, his pace slower than ever. Lagging. And then stopping altogether.

Ripper didn't want to shoot the beast, had gotten quite attached to him, didn't realize that he himself was sometimes almost as complex a character as his erstwhile partner, Michael, although, on his lonesome now (and he wasn't used to that) he was all at sixes and sevens. He missed his pard, Dack. He hated Michael.

His spirits lightened when he spotted a cluster of buildings ahead of him. He dismounted from the horse, but still held on to the reins, tugged them gently, said, 'C'mon, boy. C'mon.' The horse moved. Maybe something can be done about that leg, Ripper thought.

He didn't know the settlement. Just a cluster of buildings off a narrow trail. A small booze-den. A small livery stables which Ripper visited first, purposely keeping his eyes averted from the gently swinging sign over the single door of the hostelry.

The wizened hostler said he'd do the very best he could for the limping stallion, a fine beast worth saving. Ripper repaired to the saloon and discovered that this was a friendly settlement rather than a suspicious one as such other places were in these borderlands. Mostly Anglo, this one, too, hardcases but of a jovial sort.

Recognizing him as one of their own sort they made way for him at the bar, saying he was the first weary saddle-tramp they'd seen in a coon's age. None of them were old and they all seemed pretty well britched. Owlhooters, Ripper figured. Obviously Michael hadn't passed this way. Did he know of this place?

The beer was cold and the rye wasn't bad, and Ripper began to get merry and optimistic. To hell with

Michael, he thought. Killing Michael wouldn't bring friend Dack back, might send Ripper to join him, in fact. To hell with the boodle too! I ought to be able to get together with some of these boys, Ripper reflected optimistically, at least I'd have some back-up if it got to be I needed it.

He was told that the settlement, which didn't seem to have a name, did, however, have a resident whore. She had a crib behind the saloon, in among the privies. His new-found friends didn't know whether he'd be able to find it, however, or so they affirmed, so an entourage led him on a staggering way through the back door of the saloon and out into what, to his booze-dazed eyes, resembled a tumble-down chicken run — complete with stalking chickens.

Honey-Bedalia (there was a name to conjure with) was no chicken but had a plump figure, curly blonde hair and a milky-white skin through being out of the sun a lot. She had more tricks than a performing pony, many of which were wasted on Ripper, however, who went to sleep halfway through the proceedings.

He woke up to find himself seated in one of the privies, his pants still around his ankles. Putting himself to rights, he made his way back into the saloon. There he was told that Honey-Bedelia had another client, a regular who turned up at regular times and stayed regular times, even had a stopwatch he'd stolen from a long-distance runner and his trainer who had turned up too at Honey's crib during one of the regular's regular times.

Alhough he didn't believe half of it, Ripper took the badinage all in good part. Hell an' brimstone, he was gonna like this place!

* * *

Michael got a dirty woollen *serape* from some Mexican sheep-herders he met, with their meandering flock. They were alarmed at the half-naked man riding up at them with a rifle and belt-gun and not much else.

Michael wasn't sure whether these *peons* and their bleating charges were the same bunch he'd seen before. He didn't want to draw too much attention to himself so he acted nice: a handsome bucko, he was good at this.

The fresh air seemed to have done his shoulder wound a heap of good. He had a good horse, weapons and ammunition, but no money. He traded a pair of Mexican spurs that Don Esteban had left on the horse and the *peon* who offered the *serape* certainly got the best of the bargain, his gabbling friends gathering round him to admire his glittering spike-rowelled treasure while the stinking woollies bleated as if they'd got a bargain too. Michael, sickened by the smell (any cowman would be, he decided) and the gibberish, moved on his way.

The night fell quickly and the temperature was suddenly less. Michael was glad of the *serape* which covered him like a blanket. It was a pity it stank so much! He saw the lights of a small settlement in the distance. He didn't know whether he knew this place.

Anticipating water and eats, the horse quickened his pace. At first Michael gave him his head but then slowed him. Don't know what I'm getting into, he thought. But at this juncture both he and the horse spotted the narrow creek, like a silver snake. The horse must have smelled it. Michael couldn't smell anything but the *serape*, couldn't even smell the well-driven horse any more. I'll bivouac here till early light, he thought.

He dismounted. He and the horse drank. Michael lay down on grass and loosened the *serape*. A chill desert breeze right off the badlands hit him. He pulled the *serape* round him again and finally slid off into an odorous slumber.

He didn't have a hat. To get a hat when he got the *serape* he would have had to shoot it from a Mexican head: those sheepherders had been mighty attached to their hats, as they would well be. Michael had suffered the sun. The night breeze cooled him and he slept like a baby.

He woke with the sun in his face but not too hot yet. He told himself he felt fine. And the horse looked perky and raring to go.

To protect himself from the greater heat of the day before, Michael had ridden for a time with the *serape* pulled up over his head. He wasn't aiming to ride into the settlement looking like that, though!

The horse had a drink. Michael had a drink, then he mounted up and they made for the quiet buildings, small noises coming out to meet them as they got nearer.

21

Cal Ripper had a breakfast of steak and bacon, *frijoles* in a sweet savoury sauce, hotcakes, *tortillas* with a piquant but unidentifiable mixture of herbs, plum and apple pie, lashings of coffee and some bourbon that had been imported from upstate someplace.

The cook was a fat Mexican with deft fingers and a womanish manner and he seemed to be the only Mexican in the place. The proprietor was a Dutchman with a funny accent. Everybody called him Bunk, though Ripper couldn't figure why. The cook was called Popol, the best damn' cook he had tried in years, Ripper said, the breakfast, too. He was beginning to realize that this scruffy settlement wasn't quite what it seemed.

These folks lived high on the hog, but didn't make a show of it. This was a hideout, and if the hideouters wanted something more elaborate for celebration they could visit El Paso or San Antone, providing no law was looking for them thereabouts, of course.

Ripper leaned back in his chair and smoked a long, prime cheroot in contentment. The sun came through a nearby window in a slanting way and the breakfast saloon was redolently and not too noisily a-bustle.

A feller whom he had met the night before passed him, said 'Good morning' and halted, leaned, smoking a cigar the twin of Ripper's and looking out of the window.

The man suddenly said, 'What the hell is this?'

Ripper, feeling fine, rose and joined him, followed his gaze, peered through the glass, froze. His first glance had made him want to laugh and echo the other man's words. But suddenly nothing seemed as funny as it looked, not by a long sight.

A man was riding down the street on

a fine horse. A Mexican-looking horse with an elaborate, high-backed saddle. The man wore a scruffy-looking *serape*, but he was no Mexican. He wore no sombrero either, was bareheaded.

'That's somebody I used to know,' Ripper said: an understatement.

'I've never seen him before,' said the other man. 'A queer duck, huh?'

'I guess,' said Ripper. 'His name is Michael Tagwell.'

They both then saw the other rider coming off the trail and into the narrow, rutted main street, the only real street in the settlement. He came more quickly than the man in the *serape*, but then slowed down.

The two men saw the second man more clearly then — and the feller who stood beside Ripper said, 'I don't know the queer duck, but I know this other one. Saw him kill a man in El Paso coupla years ago. Straight, stand-up gunfight. Other feller was called Angel . . .'

'I heard about that,' said Ripper

dully. His good morning was coming to pieces around him.

'Fancied hisself as a pistolero, Angel did. Had a chance I guess, just wasn't good enough — against the fastest man with a gun I've ever seen. That's him. That's Joe Pilgrim.'

'I know that too,' said Ripper.

Michael Tagwell had halted his steed. The two men in the saloon didn't know whether Pilgrim had called out to him or not: they hadn't heard anything.

The saloon-noise behind them was intensifying. Anyway, maybe Michael had sensed he was being tailed. He stopped his horse and turned in the saddle, but slowly as if not to appear too abrupt.

He turned the horse about.

He got down from the saddle, still appearing slow.

But at the same time he was taking the elegant-looking rifle from its saddle scabbard.

He shrugged his way out of the floppy *serape* and let it fall to the ground, and then he was naked from the waist upwards.

⋆ ⋆ ⋆

Pilgrim dismounted carefully, his eyes on Michael all the time. He said, 'Don't try to lift the rifle — you won't make it.'

'I'm not going to try, Joe,' said Michael.

They faced each other. Michael lowered the rifle slowly to the ground while, thumbs hooked in belt, Pilgrim watched him. They were both erect now, remained that way almost soldier-like, as they moved a little further away from their horses.

In the saloon, Ripper whispered, 'That Michael! Always the one for the grandstand play. And Pilgrim's playing along with him.'

Ripper wanted to run, to get away while he had the chance. But he couldn't move. He had seen Michael in action. But he knew Pilgrim's reputation. Hadn't the man standing next to

189

him at this window testified to that? And now others, sensing entertainment, free at that, were crowding forward to take a look.

'Don't try it,' Pilgrim said. 'You've got a wounded shoulder.'

'Doesn't bother me,' said Michael. 'It ain't on my good side. I can take you, Joe.'

'No, I've got to take you. Take you back to pay in full for the things you've done.'

'I did what I wanted to do. I always have. Take me!'

Michael reached for the gun that was tucked into the waistband of his pants, an easy draw.

His good shoulder. His good right hand.

Smooth. Fast.

But not fast enough.

Pilgrim's draw was as fluid. Just a split second faster than the other man's. But making all the difference. The difference between life and death.

But Michael Tagwell did not die.

He took the bullet in his shoulder. His good shoulder. It bored through and the impact knocked him backwards, his gun paraboling, glinting in the morning sun before it hit the rutted sod.

He fell towards his horse, making the beast shy. But Michael did not reach those warm flanks. He collapsed on his back and the dust rose thinly about him.

He scrabbled around in a sort of desperation.

Joe Pilgrim stood with his gun half-lowered, and he didn't yet move again.

The smoke trailed thinly from the muzzle of the gun and disappeared.

Michael hauled himself to his feet. Then he did a surprising and reckless thing. He swung, staggered, ran.

Pilgrim raised the gun, levelled it, but then lowered it again. Michael disappeared into the narrow alley at the side of the saloon and Joe, gun swinging in his hand, went after him.

The saloon wasn't a big building, didn't go far back. When Pilgrim reached his end of the alley, Michael, despite his wound, moving fast, was going round the corner at the other end. He had been running with wild instinct and, following him, Pilgrim had to tread carefully to negotiate the beaten, uneven soil and the various items of rubbish with which it was garnished.

At the top of the alley he stumbled and that was when, surprisingly, Michael came at him. Around the corner. With something swinging in his left hand. A pick-axe he had picked up by its broken handle, which, however, had enough wood left for him to be able to grip it, swing it ferociously.

There wasn't much room and one wickedly sharp side of the pick-axe caught the wooden wall and was deflected. It was a side of the rusty steel that caught Pilgrim on his right arm, numbing it, making him drop his gun, lurch past Michael and out into the open beyond the back end of the alley.

Turning, Michael raised the pick-axe again over his head ready to swing it down powerfully in a last murderous blow.

He was caught in a frozen tableau as a bullet bored into the side of his head and the gunshot was like an echo. He slammed back against the edge of the wall behind him and he dropped the pick-axe and fell, rolled until he was face-down and then became still.

Pilgrim clambered to his feet, retrieving his gun as he did so, pouching it.

Cal Ripper stood outside the back door of the saloon with a smoking gun in his hand, the thin black thread slowly dispelling.

'I'm mighty indebted to you,' Pilgrim said.

'I owed him,' Ripper said.

Another man joined Ripper, his friend who had stood beside him at a window at front of the saloon and watched the dramatic tableau outside.

Other men crowded out now, peering, gesticulating, questioning.

Pilgrim said, 'I was supposed to take you back.'

Cal Ripper's friend said, 'He ain't goin' anyplace with you, Joe Pilgrim. He's one of us now an' he's staying right here.'

Ripper said, 'I'm a robber, Joe, not a killer. I had no hand in killing . . . '

His voice tailed off. Under the circumstances, Pilgrim could find little to say to this. No question. No answer. He was a courageous man but not a man to throw his life away foolishly. The life that Cal Ripper had given back to him. Killer or not, Ripper had plenty friends with guns, though he'd already pouched his own.

Pilgrim smiled thinly, bowed slightly, mockingly.

'So be it, gents,' he said.

Cal Ripper pointed at the bloodied half-naked body, said, 'My friends will bury that.'

'You backed the wrong nag, huh?'

'I shore as hell did.'

'I'll take the horse. It belongs to somebody else.'

Yes, he had to take the horse back. And he'd got to pick up a boodle-bundle which had been thrown down on the floor of a ruined line hut as if it were so much garbage.

★ ★ ★

The three *compadres* separated. The old man to 'go home' as he wearily put it, the two younger ones to go in the other direction, taking the longer trail.

As the two rode, Pilgrim said, 'I've got to make a call before we get home.'

'As you wish, *amigo*,' said Lean Luke.

22

As night began to fall and they were passing through the low range of hills a few miles from the Teller ranch, they were stopped by three riders who came out of concealment with guns drawn. All three were older than Joe Pilgrim and Luke Profett and though they were determined-looking, purposeful, they didn't look or act like gunfighters, the sort that the younger pair both knew so well.

The one who appeared to be the leader of the trio asked, 'What are you doing in this territory?'

Pilgrim said, 'We're making for the Teller place. Pete and Arabella are good friends of mine. My name is Joe Pilgrim and this is my friend, Luke Profett. What's happening?'

'Nothing's happening yet,' said the older man. 'The Tellers have spoken of you. Come along.'

More folks were gathered at the ranch as Joe and Arabella came out to meet the party. Light spilled out onto the yard and the greensward. The girl's eyes shone as Pilgrim dismounted and faced her. He caught her by her shoulders and looked into her face.

Pilgrim introduced Luke, and Pete and his daughter shook the lean young man by the hand and greeted him, though Pete had to add that the two new arrivals had not turned up at a happy time. He put Pilgrim quickly in the picture.

There had been more trouble from the Eastern combination that literally wanted to take over this territory. A discovery had been made of where the now more aggressive bunch hung out and it looked as if they were planning an all-out attack on the ranches and smallholdings.

The folks of the gentle hills and the valley lands had decided to get together and act first. This was their night.

'That bunch have gunfighters,' one of the ranchers said. 'But we ain't exactly slouches. All of us. Some of us fought Injuns on this land in the old days.'

'I'll come with you,' said Joe Pilgrim.

'This ain't your put-in, son,' said Pete Teller.

'It is now,' said Pilgrim, and Arabella and he exchanged glances and, momentarily it was as if there was nobody else around.

'Where Joe goes I go,' said Luke Profett.

'All right,' said Pete, resignedly. He added, 'We aim to try and take that bunch by surprise and avoid bloodshed. We've already got scouts watching that place.'

Pilgrim once again met the Tellers' two young hands, Pink and Seal. They had tossed a coin to see who would stay with Arabella, although she said she didn't need anybody and, in fact, would be quite ready to join the raiding party, adding that she could be as good as most of 'em and better maybe than some.

Most of the womenfolk, were ensconced in one of the bigger ranchhouses, but Arabella had already elected to stay where she was. Laughter was forced when Pete Teller said in a not-too-soft aside to Pilgrim, 'You're going to have trouble with that girl, mark my words on it,' admitting, it seemed, he knew full well how things were with his daughter and the young gunfighter whose put-in would be very valuable. And Pilgrim's lean, watchful pardner looked as if he could well handle himself.

They all moved out and the girl and her bodyguard, young Pink, watched them go.

Joe Pilgrim didn't have his bulging twin-saddle-bags with him; they were in a locked cupboard in the Teller place. He was unencumbered, his trail weariness gone from him and ready to meet whatever what was before him.

It was a ghost town but there were lights there. There were guards which the ranchers' scouts had spotted. They were pretty sure they themselves hadn't been spotted, though.

Pilgrim said to Pete Teller, 'I remember my old man mentioning a scheme he and some Pinkerton men worked during a range war in the Dakotas. Have we got plenty of rope?'

'I reckon,' said Pete. 'We're cowmen, son. We've all got *reatas*. And plenty more besides, I shouldn't wonder.'

'We've got to fix those guards first. Luke an' me will do that.'

'Did I hear my name spoken in vain?' queried the nearby lean man, urging his horse nearer.

'Right, *amigo*. Listen up.'

A trickle of hissing stream, too narrow and shallow to be called a creek, in a hollow where the sound of hooves would be blanketed from the town, clouds blanketing the moon. A great night for prowling and skulduggery.

Men waiting on edge.

Pilgrim and Luke leaving their horses.

The scouts had figured on only three guards at most. That gang figured they were sitting pretty till they got ready to move!

Like crouching ghosts, Pilgrim and Luke split up, going in different directions, half-circling.

The badlands lay behind the town. In the old days, the boys had been told, gold had been found in this territory. But the strain had been a fool's pocket and had petered out and the gimcrack buildings which had been built on the edge of the wastelands had petered out with it.

Grass in front, but not enough for good cowmen and their beef, and even less for any benighted cuss who fancied sheep.

A town of ghosts.

But the two-legged things that the two gunfighters sought were not ghosts.

Lights had gone out, except for one bright one way back a little. A light in the old saloon. Pilgrim heard a slight sound and then he spotted his man; crouched, moved eel-like.

The burly guard was taken completely by surprise, had no chance to raise his butt-grounded rifle or reach for his belt-gun.

Pilgrim's strong left hand closed around his throat and squeezed. The man gurgled but, before he could make a louder sound, his attacker's gun-barrel whipped him across the temple and he sagged.

Pilgrim lowered him gently to the ground like a sleeping babe, gently breathing. This was a gink who had just being doing a job he was paid for. His attacker had himself done similar jobs in the past. There should be no noise and, if possible, no killing. This attacker was tired of killing.

Pilgrim had come well prepared, however. He gagged the unconscious man with a worn kerchief, balled, tied then with a strip of rag. He tied the man's wrists with rawhide.

He turned off towards the left, to the approximate place where his partner Luke would be.

He heard a cry, soon muffled, not loud enough anyway to give any kind of alarm. When he reached Luke, the lean man was trussing the unconscious guard like a turkey with his jib well-stuffed.

Together they ranged the front perimeter of the ghost town.

'Must've been only two right now,' said Pilgrim. 'And I guess some of the boys will be round back by now.'

'I'll bring the others in,' Luke said, and he moved out into the greater dark.

Pilgrim made a slow zig-zag progress forward. A quiet, determined man, alone, creeping in the night, could do a lot of damage.

He crouched in a concertina'd structure that smelled as if it had once been a privy as he saw the fires spring up out back on the edge of the badlands. The small party out there had made good with their torches.

The rapidly spreading blobs of fire were spotted and in the bigger building in the centre of the ghost town, shouting voices gave the alarm. There was bewilderment in the sound.

Luke would have reached the horsemen in the dip by now and they would be descending in force on the front of the town. In line, like a well-trained regiment charging — old Pete would see to that. And the long rope, tied lengths, taut, stretched between men and horses.

In the town, men were running towards the strips of conflagrations on the edge of the badlands. But the fire-raisers, Pilgrim knew, would be racing round to the front to join the rest of the ranchers' army.

Out back, the fires were lessening. Water was being used no doubt. Near to the big, lighted building — and the lights were getting brighter — somebody was yelling orders. There was a clatter of horses' hooves.

But now, from the front, there was a veritable thunder of hooves.

A man ran towards Pilgrim from the direction of the hammering hooves. The third guard maybe. Pilgrim came out of concealment and swung his handgun like a whip. The barrel hit the running man on the side of his head with a satisfying clunk and he fell like a well-chopped tree and lay still.

Pilgrim sank into partial concealment again. He didn't want to be attacked in the night by one of his own. He hoped Luke remembered to bring his damn' horse, the cheery pinto, who would enjoy himself in the way his master was enjoying himself now, in peril though he undoubtedly was. Men seemed to be all around him, but now most of them were horsed, and that was a good thing.

Even so, Pilgrim was suddenly spotted by a man on a horse who, eyes wide, unrecognizing, wheeled the mount in a spurt of dust.

Pilgrim didn't wait for him to make

up his mind but grabbed the nearest leg and hauled the man down to the ground like a sack of meal. The feller was no easy target though, was big and brawny. They tussled like two wrestling bears.

His hands gripped Pilgrim's throat. The big body pinned him so hard he was unable to raise his gun and use it as a club. He butted the man in the face with his head, felt the nose snap. Then blood gushed into Pilgrim's face and the crawlike grip on his throat was relaxed.

Pilgrim, free, lurched backwards. His gun hand was loose and again he used the weapon with telling effect, no hammer, no trigger. But hammerlike, laying his big opponent out and useless.

Pilgrim's way was clear. He made his way to the still lit bigger building and in the doorway ran into a tall young man — who he could have best described as a fancy-pants — who reached for a gun in a shoulder holster but desisted when Pilgrim poked his own Colt into a lean belly.

'Back up, bucko,' Pilgrim said, and the fancy-pants backed up. He certainly had nobody else to back him up: the building was empty. As if all the ghosts had fled. And outside, the sounds of strife had moved further away.

Pilgrim made the young man, who looked like a fancy Easterner, turn about, reached over his shoulder and took his natty derringer, then made him sit on a rocky chair. The place looked as if it had been made habitable, but it was no palace.

'Who are you?' the young man asked.

'Makes no difference now. You're finished, bucko. You left things a mite too late. All you've got to worry about is whether my rancher friends figure to string you up from the nearest tall tree.'

Outside, the ominous sounds were getting less.

'Joe?' a voice called.

'In here.'

Lean Luke came in with Pete Teller just behind him.

'Well, hello, Mr Carstairs.'

'Mr Teller,' said the fancy boy courteously, but looking apprehensive.

Pete didn't beat around in the undergrowth but went right to the point. 'I want you to take a message back to your Eastern bosses. Your boys are beaten. They ain't about to fight your battles any more.' The older man's eyes twinkled as he exchanged glances with Pilgrim. 'Went down like a row of skittles . . . '

'Any hurts?'

'Some on both sides, but nobody killed.'

'You hear that, bucko?'

'I hear.' Carstairs looked relieved.

'Think yourself lucky, you an' your people. And you hear what this man said to you.'

'There'll be no more trouble,' Carstairs said.

'Some of your boys are gone already,' Pete Teller said. 'We'll let the rest go, by and by.'

'I will go. I'll do as you say. I am

pretty sure my people will listen. They
didn't want this in the first place.
But . . . '

'Cut it,' snarled Pilgrim. 'Or my
friend might change his mind.'

Carstairs began to rise. 'All right,' he
said.

★   ★   ★

They sat licking their wounds. The
waters of the narrow stream helped.
Nobody too badly hurt which, in itself,
was like a small miracle.

An old man whom Pilgrim had heard
called Jobey, just Jobey, was tying a
bandage around a wounded ankle and
said, 'Mebbe you boys oughta make me
a *travois*.'

Pete Teller laughed. 'Like hell we will.
You'll fork your hoss same as all of us.'

'I guess.' Jobey laughed too. 'Funny
thing is, as I told you, Pete, I was
aiming to sell my place anyway — it
ain't been the same since my Ella died
— and I was gonna move to Kansas

and live with my daughter and her hubby an' the two grandchildren. But I wasn't goin' to sell to those goddamn bullies. I do still want to sell, though.'

There was a small silence. Then Joe Pilgrim said, 'I'd like to take you up on that, suh. But me an' my pard, Luke here' — a jerk of thumb in the direction of the lean man who had acquitted himself so well this night — 'have to go up-country first to deliver somep'n an' put things right.'

'I can wait,' said Jobey.

Meaningful glances now seemed to be the order of the night and Joe Pilgrim and Pete Teller exchanged yet another one. And the older man grinned.

'I know somebody else who'll wait, too,' he said.